Henry De Vere Stacpoole

Death, the Knight, and the Lady

Henry De Vere Stacpoole

Death, the Knight, and the Lady

ISBN/EAN: 9783743400047

Manufactured in Europe, USA, Canada, Australia, Japa

Cover: Foto ©Andreas Hilbeck / pixelio.de

Manufactured and distributed by brebook publishing software (www.brebook.com)

Henry De Vere Stacpoole

Death, the Knight, and the Lady

DEATH THE KNIGHT AND THE LADY

DEATH THE KNIGHT

AND THE LADY

A GHOST STORY

BY

H. DE VERE STACPOOLE

JOHN LANE

THE BODLEY HEAD

LONDON & NEW YORK

MDCCCXCVII

CONTENTS

BALLAD OF THE ARRAS

Lo ! where are now these armoured hosts
Mailed for the tourney *cāp-a-pie*,
These dames and damozelles whose ghosts
Make of the past this pagentry ?

O sanguine book of History !
Romance with perfume cloaks thy must,
But he who shakes the page may see
—Dust.

Stiff hangs the arras in the gloom ;
I turn my head awhile to gaze :
Here lordly stallions fret and fume,
Here streams o'er briar and brake the chase.

Here sounds a horn, here turns a face,
How filled with fires of life and lust !
Wind shakes the arras and betrays
—Dust.

Ephemeral hand inditing this
Great hound that lolls against my knee,
Lips pursed in thought as if to kiss
Regret—full soon the time must be.

When one shall search, but find not ye,
For that dim moth whose labours rust
All forms in time or tapestry
—Dust.

Forth offspring to the perch and then
Clap wings—or fall, if find you must
This saddest fate of books or men
—Dust.

DEATH THE KNIGHT
AND THE LADY

PROLOGUE

I HAD almost forgotten James Wilder's existence, when, one night in June, I received an urgent message asking me to call upon him without delay.

An hour later I was sitting in his library, and in the arm-chair opposite mine was sunk what seemed the spectre of my friend. During the ten months that had elapsed since our last meeting he had passed from middle life to premature old age.

"I am glad you have come," he said, "I am in need of a friend, but do not speak to me yet, that is, for a moment, I wish to think."

His eyes fell from me to the carpet, he seemed watching something, and his thin lips were curled in a ghostly smile.

The room was hot and oppressive, flowers were heaped everywhere in profusion, and the large wood fire burning in the grate mixed its faint aromatic smell with the perfume of the roses and tube-roses lolling in their porcelain bowls.

I sat watching the burning logs and thinking.   I had known Wilder for some years, I had been his intimate friend, but how much did I know really about him? Not much.   I had dined with him, talked with him, exchanged opinions; I knew that he was wealthy, that he owned a house somewhere in the country, to which he never invited friends, and of which I had heard rumours needless to set down here.   That he was an opium eater I knew, and that was the extent of my knowledge of the man.

Of the being who existed behind that careworn, weary face, I knew absolutely nothing, but I had always guessed it to be occupied with some secret trouble, pressed upon by some sin or sorrow of which it dared not speak; also, by some freak of imagination, I had always coupled this imaginary sorrow of Wilder's with that house in the country of which I had received so many mysterious hints.

Suddenly I started from my reverie. Wilder was speaking.

"Ah, my dear——, I have been trying to brace myself for the effort, but I cannot, I cannot; what I have to ask of you, you will do without question if you are my friend, but to speak of it all, to go over that terrible ground, oh! impossible, impossible, impossible."

His voice died away into a whisper, and he struck with his thin hand on the arm of his chair, as if beating time to some dreary tune heard by him alone.

"What I ask of you is this, to start as soon as possible for my place in Yorkshire, and to see carried out after the fashion I desire, the obsequies of a man—I mean, a woman—who is lying there dead."

Again his voice sank to a whisper, his eyes turned from mine evasively, and he covered them with one of his thin white hands.

A man—I mean a woman—what *did* he mean?

" Will you do this? "

" Yes, I will do as you ask ; it seems strange, no matter, I will do it."

" You take a load from me. Ah, my dear ——, if you could only guess what I have suffered, the terrors, the tortures, the *nameless* misery. I ought to be at the grave side when this terrible burial—Oh, how my head wanders, I have scarcely the power of thought, but say it once again, you will do what I ask, promise me that again."

" Yes, yes, I promise, set your mind at rest —I will do what you require."

" You will start, then, at once? "

" To-morrow."

" Yes, to-morrow early, to-morrow early ; and now as to what you are to do. Listen, at Ashworth, near my place, there lives a man who works in granite, you will get him to cut a memorial tablet. These words are to be upon it, they are written on this piece of paper, take it; the body is to be buried in the vault of the little church in the park; remember it is to be interred dressed exactly as I have ordered it to be dressed, this is my chief reason for asking you to attend the last ceremonies. I dare not leave this matter to the hands of servants, and I— may not go myself, I am broken down with ill-health and sorrow, and the journey would kill me, though, indeed, I am dying fast enough."

His eyes were wandering again, as if following some imaginary spectre about the room. I looked at the piece of paper, on it was written—

"SIR GERALD WILDER, Knt.
Rest in Peace."

Sir Gerald Wilder! why, a moment ago he said "a woman." What mystery was in this? And then, "Rest in Peace," it sounded like a command.

"The coffin is ordered," broke out Wilder, suddenly seeming to return to this world from the world of his imagination. "The coffin is made, promise me again, you will go."

"I will go."

The next morning I started for Ashworth, in Yorkshire, to fulfil my strange mission. I had asked no more of Wilder, content to act without question, which is the first office of friendship. I started early, and arrived at Ashworth shortly after three o'clock. A carriage was waiting to take me to the Gables. The weather was exquisite, and the moors over which the white road led us stretched on either side, far as the eye could reach, like a rolling sea under the blue summer sky and hot June sun. The rocking motion sent me to sleep. When I woke the wheels were crashing on gravel, and the carriage was passing swiftly through a long, dark avenue.

This was, then, the Gables, this great old-fashioned gloomy house, with a broad portico supported on fluted granite pillars, facing the broad park dotted with clumps of trees, so broad and so far-reaching that the deer in the furthermost parts were reduced to moving specks.

The door was opened by an ill-looking servant-maid, whose sour and crabbed face struck an unpleasant note against the old-fashioned and romantic surroundings.

The great hall, oak-panelled, and lit by stained glass windows, hid amongst its other treasures an echo, whose dreamy voice repeated my footsteps with a sound like the pattering of a ghost. I stood for a moment, my heart absorbing the silence of this place, so far removed from the spirit of to-day. The air held something, I know not what, it seemed like an odour left from the perfumed robes of Romance.

I heard a sound behind me, and turning, I saw an old servant man with silvery white hair. He showed me to my room, and I kept him whilst I explained fully my business.

He listened respectfully, but like a person who had ceased to take any interest in life. When I had finished, I asked him to take me to the room where the dead person lay.

He led the way down a corridor, opened

a door, and stood aside whilst I entered.
I found myself in a bedroom hung with
rose-coloured silk; the window was open,
and through it came the warm evening
breeze and the far-off cawing of rooks.

On the bed I saw a form, but I could
scarcely believe that what I saw was real.
Stretched upon the snow-white coverlet lay
the body of a cavalier, full-dressed in amber
satin doublet and long buff-coloured riding-
boots, his hair long, curling, and black as
night, surrounded a face pale as marble and
beautiful as a woman's.   His white right
hand, peeping from its lace ruffle, grasped
the hilt of a sword, his left hand grasped
a silver trumpet.   Attached to the trumpet
a crimson silk cord streaked the coverlet
like a thin and tortuous stream of blood.
He seemed to have stepped from the pages
of romance, and to have laid himself down
here to rest.   I trembled as I looked, feared
to stir lest he should wake, yet I well knew
him to be dead.   I might have fancied myself in a dream but for the far-off clamour
of the rooks coming through the evening

sky outside and the sound of my own heart beating.

Was it a man? was it a woman? the face might have done for either, yet it was the most beautiful face I had ever beheld, the most romantic, the most pathetic. Then recollection woke up, and I shuddered. This, then, was Sir Gerald Wilder. This form, more beautiful than a picture, was the sorrow of James Wilder, the thing that had driven him to opium, the thing that had broken his heart and crowned him with premature old age. How? Why? I dared scarcely think.

I stole from the room. In the passage I found the old man-servant waiting for me; he shut the door softly, and I followed him back to my own room. There I took his arm and looked in his face.

" What is the meaning of this? "

" I dursn't tell you, sir; oh, sir, my heart be gone with the sorrow of it all, but if you wish, I will bring the book that he was always a-writing in for these months past."

" Yes, get the book, please, at once: no

thank you, nothing to eat yet, I wish to see the book first."

He went, and returned with a large, old-fashioned common-place book, the leaves of which were covered with writing. It was a woman's hand.

I took it down stairs, and went with it into the garden.

There, on a seat in the middle of an old Dutch garden, very prim, very silent, where the sunlight fell upon the faces of the amber and purple pansies, and the great white carnations shook their ruffles to the wind with a dreamy and seventeenth century air, I sat and read this story, written by the hand of a dead cavalier who craves, through me, your sympathy for his deathless sorrow.

THE BOOK

CHAPTER I

I DESCRIBE MYSELF

I CANNOT tell you my story unless I tell you who I am and what I am. Oh, it is not for pleasure that I am writing all this down, but just because I—must.

My name is Beatrice Sinclair, and I am the last representative of an old and ruined family. There were Sinclairs in the time of King Charles who were great people at Court—you must accept the statement, for I cannot write much about this family of mine, the very thought of it fills me with a kind of horror. What would all those men with long flowing hair, those women with patches on their faces,—what would they say if they could see me, the last of their race, and could know what I have been?

Perhaps you guess what I mean, perhaps you are sneering at me; you can do so if you please, for I am˙ so very ill that I care for nothing now, and they say I am dying. I know now, oh, I know well why an animal crawls away and hides itself to die: though I am only twenty-three I know more about death than those Egyptians who have been shut up in pyramids alone with him for a thousand years.

From the window where I am sitting now, wrapped up in shawls, I can see the garden; the frost has gone, and I can see a yellow crocus that has pushed its head up through the dark, stiff mould. If it knew what I know of life, it would draw that head back.

You must think me a very gloomy person, and indeed just now I am, for I am thinking of a part of my history of which I shall not speak, but only hint.

Some time, no matter how long ago, I was living at the Bath Hotel. I had plenty of clothes and money, and I thought I was in love. Well, one day I found myself deserted, I found a letter on the breakfast table enclosing a blue strip of paper—a cheque for two hundred pounds. I did not scream and tear my hair as a girl I know said she did when she was deserted, I believe I laughed.

I went to the theatre that night alone, and everybody stared at me. I was beautiful then, I am nearly as beautiful now, but it was only on that night that I first fully recognised how beautiful I was, I could see it in the faces of the men who looked at me, and in the manner of the women,—how women hate one another! and yet some women have been very good to me.

Well, when I got home I found supper waiting for me, and after supper I looked at myself again in the long pier glass opposite the fireplace ; then a strange feeling came over me that I had never felt before, I felt a thirst to be admired, I say thirst, for it was so, it was really in the back of my throat that this feeling came, but it was in my head as well ; it was not the admiration of ordinary people that I wanted ; I craved to see some being as lovely as myself turn its head to gaze at me.

Oh! my beautiful face, how I loved you, oh! the nights I have woken up shivering to think of the dissecting rooms where they take the bodies of the people who have no friends.

At the end of six months my two hundred pounds were nearly gone. I lived innocently, I lived in a kind of dream. Men filled me with a kind of horror, when they looked at me in the streets I shuddered ; I shudder still, and I wonder why God ever made such a blind and cruel thing as man.

I moved into furnished rooms : all this is misty now in my mind. If I had died then I might never have gone to heaven, but I would never have seen hell. I got typhoid fever ; my rings lay on the dressing table, hoops of sapphires and emeralds ; each fortnight a ring went to pay for my rooms and the doctor, who seemed never able to cure me.

I cannot tell you much after this, I can only say that I struggled, mad with pride and mad with hatred. I starved, but why should I pain you, and make more sad a story that is already sad enough?

CHAPTER II

JAMES WILDER

IT is about six months ago. I was in a very bad way. I was walking along the south side of Russell Square one day— the 17th of September I remember now— and thinking to myself how I should pay my landlady the three weeks' rent owing to her.

Deeply as I was trying to think I could not help noticing a man coming towards me, striding along with his hat tilted back from his forehead, his head in the air, and looking just like a person walking in his sleep. I made way to let him pass, then suddenly I felt him grasp me by the arm and I heard him say " Ah ! "

I knew at once—how shall I put it— that he only wanted to speak to me, that he had mistaken me for someone he knew, and as I looked in his face I did not feel a bit afraid, although his face was strange enough, goodness knows.

"What is your name?" he asked.

"Jane Seymour," I replied, for it was my name, at least the name I went under.

"Ah!" he said, and his hand fell from my arm. I never saw a person look so disappointed as he looked just then; I heard him muttering something like "always the same, disappointment, death," then he turned to go, and I broke into tears.

I was hungry and I had no money; he had seemed almost friendly, and now he was going — I could scarcely speak, I leaned up against the railings, I remember trying to hide a hole in my glove, for I had determined on telling him my real name.

"Well?" he said, "Well?"

"My name is Beatrice Sinclair," I answered; "that is my real name."

Then I stopped crying, for I was

absolutely frightened, *such* a change came over this strange man ; two large tears ran down his face, he clasped his hands together with the fingers across the backs of each hand, and I thought for one moment that he was a lunatic, then somehow I *knew* that he was not.

"Beatrice Sinclair," he muttered to me in a low voice, as if afraid of someone else hearing him, "Beatrice Sinclair, oh, Beatrice! the time I have been searching for you, the three weary years, the nights of terror ; but it is over now, thank God ! thank God."

I felt very strange as he said all this. I knew well that this man was not in love with me; I had no relations, so he could not be a relation, and yet I knew in a horribly certain kind of manner that he knew me, that he had been searching for me, and—had found me.

A hansom cab was passing, he hailed it and we both got in, then I heard him giving directions to the driver, "No.—Berkeley Square," he said, "and drive quick."

"You look pale and sick," that was the

only thing he said during our drive. But the way in which he said it was very queer. He did not seem in the least to care whether I was pale or sick, and yet he had seemed so glad to find me, " Can he be mad after all ? " thought I.

The cab stopped at a large house in Berkeley Square, and we got out ; he gave the driver half-a-sovereign, and without waiting for the change went up the steps, and opened the door with a latch-key ; " Come on," he said, beckoning to me, and I followed.

We entered a great hall with a floor of polished oak ; I saw jars of flowers standing here and there, and idols half hidden by palms and long feathery grasses.

He opened a door and motioned me to enter a room, and I went in, feeling horrible in my shabby clothes amongst all this splendour.

It was a library. He told me to sit down, and I sat in a great easy-chair, looking about me whilst he went to a window, and stood for nearly a minute looking out, jingling money in his pocket, but not speaking a word.

—Oh, this writing makes my head ache so, and this cough, cough, cough, that tears me from morning till night!—

Well, he stood at the window without speaking, and I kept trying to hide my boots under my skirt; but I looked about me, and noticed everything in the room at the same time.

The books were all set in narrow bookcases, and between the bookcases there were spaces occupied by pictures, and I never had seen such strange pictures before. They were just like pictures of ghosts, beautiful faces nearly all of them, but they seemed like faces made out of mist, if you understand me. Over the mantelpiece stood a portrait of an old man with grey hair, and on the gold frame of this picture was written in black letters the name, "Swedenborg."

At last my companion turned from the window, wheeled a chair close to me, and sat down.

"Now," he said, "I want you to tell me all you know about your family. I want to make perfectly sure that you *are* the person for whom I have been seeking. Tell me unreservedly, it will be to your advantage."

He had taken his gloves off now, and I saw that his hands, very white and delicate-looking, were absolutely covered with the most exquisite rings.

"Mine is a very old family," I said. "We lived once in a castle in the North of England, Castle Sinclair."

"Yes, yes."

"My father was an officer. He was very extravagant. He died in India. I was sent to school in England, then I became a governess—then—then—"

"You need not tell me the rest," he said, "I know it. Yes, you are indeed Beatrice Sinclair." He looked at me in a gloomy manner. Then "You have spoken frankly," he said, "and I shall do the same. My name is James Wilder."

He paused, and looked at me hard, but I said nothing.

"Ah!" he continued, "you know nothing of the past, then? Perhaps it is better so, but I must tell you some of it, so that you may do what I require you to do. Listen. In the reign of King Charles the First a terrible tragedy happened. A member of the Wilder family did a fearful wrong upon a member of the Sinclair family. No family feud took place, because Gerald Wilder, who had committed this wrong, expiated it by suicide, but a blind, reasonless, unintentional feud has been going on between the two houses ever since. The house of Sinclair has warred with our family in a strange and fearful manner. All the eldest sons of our house have been slain before the age of twenty by—a Sinclair. My eldest brother was slain by your father's brother."

"My father's brother?"

"Yes, they were out shooting together. My brother was shot dead by your uncle. It was an accident; no one was to blame, but fate. Now the fortunes of the two families have been altering during all these years. The house of Wilder is at its zenith.

Speaking in a worldly sense, I am worth at least fifty thousand a year, at *least*, and the house of Sinclair?—you are its last representative, how much are you worth?"

" Less than nothing."

" Let us be friends then, let us be friends," said Wilder, in a voice full of supplication. How strange it sounded to hear a man like this, wealthy and great, asking for *my* friendship. " Let us be friends,—the two last representatives of these great houses must forgive each other. Love can heal this awful wound, and the house of Wilder shall not be extinct. Oh, God is great and good, he will sanction this love even though you are what you are."

He was walking up and down the room as he spoke. " Does he want me to love *him*?" I thought."

Then he stopped.

" You have no money?"

" None."

He went to a desk and drew out a cheque-book, scribbled for a moment, tore off a cheque, and brought it to me.

I looked at it: it was a cheque on the British Linen Company's Bank for five hundred pounds. I felt just as if I were drunk, the books in the cases seemed to dance.

"This can't be for me," I remember saying; "or do you want me to do some dreadful thing, that you offer me all this money——"

I stopped, for he was smiling at me such a melancholy, kind smile, it told me at once that I had nothing to fear from him. He called me "child," and took my hand and kissed it—I felt so ashamed of my glove, but he did not seem to notice the holes in it, nor how old it was.

"Yes," he said, "the money is for you; you must buy yourself beautiful clothes and some jewellery. I am going to send you to the north of England, to do what has to be done. You must start on the day after to-morrow; have no fear, I wish you to do nothing sinful or wrong, but rather the best work mortal ever did; you shall be provided for. I will set aside a fund for you under trustees ; it is an act of piety, not charity, for in saving the last of the Sinclairs from want I am doing an act which may expiate the sin our house committed. Beatrice Sinclair, you shall never want again, never be cold or hungry."

I was crying like a child. When I could cry no more he began speaking again.

" You must stay in this house until you start, that is, if you please. My carriage shall take you to all the shops you require to visit ; by the way, spend *all* that money on clothes. I will give you a note to the jewellers with whom I deal in Bond Street, and you can supply yourself with all the jewellery you require ; don't think about the expense. You are beautiful by nature, but I wish you to be as beautiful as art can make you. Then, again, you will require dressing-bags and portmanteaux, and such things. I will give you a note to the best firm in London. I need not speak to you on matters of taste ; you are a lady— I only say this, spare no expense. Is that cheque sufficient ? "

"More than sufficient." I felt dazed and strange. Did he intend to marry me? Why was he sending me to the north of England? But it was delightful, I could not describe my feelings.

"Now you must have some food," he said, getting up and moving to the door as he spoke. "Come with me to the dining-room."

CHAPTER III

A SOUND WHICH REMINDS ME OF
MY PAST

THE table was laid for luncheon in the
dining-room, and as I took my seat at a
place he pointed out, he went to a speaking tube and whistled down it. Then I
heard him ordering the carriage to be ready
in an hour. "Will that suit you?" he asked,
looking at me.

"Yes," I replied. I was laughing now.
Oh, life had turned so in a moment from
awfulness to loveliness. I never pinched
myself to feel if I were in a dream or not.
I have read about that in stories, and I
think it's stupid, besides, I did not want to
wake up if it was a dream. I did not want
to talk either, I was too happy.

I thought of the dinner I had yesterday.

I could not remember what it was, then I remembered I had not dined yesterday at all; I had lent my last shilling to Jessie, who lives in the room below mine; she had sworn to pay me back in the evening if she was lucky, and then she came back drunk at twelve o'clock, swearing like a soldier, poor Jessie——

Wilder ate very little and spoke scarcely at all, I think the only thing he said in the way of conversation was "I never have servants in the room when I am eating;" and I said to myself, "Thank goodness." Just imagine how I would have felt if one of those dreadful men-servants had been gliding about the room,—my wristbands all frayed, my hands not very clean, for those cheap gloves dye one's hands, and my collar crumpled.

Wilder wanted to open me some champagne, but I said no. I thought he looked pleased. He had a decanter before him, and he poured himself out a glass from it.

"I don't ask you to take this," he said in an apologetic sort of manner; "because it would—well a glass of it would kill you, it's opium, I am used to it—all the worry I have had———" His head sunk on his breast, and I felt sorry for him, though he was so rich and lived in such a beautiful house. After a moment he looked up—we had finished eating.

"Gerald," he said, "I want you to be happy; poor soul, you have suffered too, but perhaps it is for the best."

"Why do you call me Gerald?" I asked, staring at him. A dreamy look had come over his strange face, perhaps it was the opium.

"Did I call you Gerald?" he said, "well, you will know why soon, I want you to be happy."

He rose from the table. "Come," he said, "I will show you to your room."

I followed him into the hall, then up a great broad staircase carpeted with soft fleecy carpet; on the first landing he opened a door.

"This is your room," he said, "you will find everything you require; when you are ready come downstairs and you will find the carriage waiting."

He shut the door on me, and I found myself alone.

It was a small, but beautifully furnished bedroom. A fire was burning in the grate; on the bed lay a great sealskin cloak, perfectly new. It was evidently intended for me, I tried it on before the glass, it reached to my feet, hiding all my shabby clothes. Then I took it off and laid it on the bed again. I looked at the floor beside the fireplace. There, in a row, stood a number of ladies' boots and shoes, different sizes; a wardrobe stood open, I looked in, dresses of dark silk and satin, bonnets, hats; on the dressing-table great ivory hair brushes, gloves, handkerchiefs, scent bottles of cut glass, a curling tongs and spirit lamp which was lit, a little strip of paper on which was written, "Help yourself to whatever you require."

I could have cried again, but somehow I didn't. I looked all round, and then I remember lifting up my arms to stretch myself, why I did so I don't know.

Then, as I began undressing, I laughed, I spoke to the things in the room just like a child, I asked questions of the little silver clock on the mantelpiece—oh, those hideous old boots I had worn so long, they seemed to make faces at me as I took them off. I flung them in a corner.

In an alcove stood a great bath ; I turned the tap, shaped like a dragon's head, and the water roared and foamed into the bath through the dragon's mouth ; I smelt the water, I tasted it, it was sea water ; in a minute the bath was full.

The luxury of it ! the warm briny water that let one's limbs float loose like seaweed. I pretended to drown myself for fun, then I turned over on my face, floating, and seized the dragon's head in both hands.

Then, as I lay floating, I listened to the far away sound I knew so well—the distant roar of carts and cabs in the streets.

I sprang out of the bath in a fury. I had never thought of it before like this, now I saw all the wretchedness that I had gone through, saw it all a million times more clearly than I had ever done when I was in it. Oh, the vile world, I could have eaten it, eaten it.

Then I caught a glimpse of my naked figure in the long glass. I was beautiful as ever, my limbs were white as snow. I whirled round, and my long black hair flew out in a mist, scattering drops of water everywhere.

Yes, I was even more beautiful than before, my troubles had given my face more expression; my teeth were perfect— Jessie's teeth were broken—*Jessie*. I would be revenged yet. I leaned on my side before the great glass, gazing at myself as gloomily as a thunder-cloud. I would be revenged on this world. Why had God created such a place, and the clergymen whining about heaven, and the doctors who took a poor girl's rings, and—I smelt a subtle perfume, and turning, I saw a great bunch of violets standing in a little bowl in the corner.

I don't know why, but they made me feel choky, and I remember taking them to me and kissing them, and putting them back.

Then I dried myself in a huge towel, and dressed. I laughed at the curling tongs, and blew the little lamp out—my hair did not want curling tongs. I laughed to think of the frights of women going about with their noses in the air, who had to curl their heads.

One of the bonnets in the wardrobe fitted me perfectly. I could have chosen a hat, but I preferred this bonnet. I put on the sealskin cloak. Then, taking the bunch of violets with the stalks all dripping, I put it in my breast.

Wilder was standing in the hall as I came down the great staircase. He smiled at the violets as if he were pleased. "You look very well," he said, passing, as he spoke, into the library, where I followed him. "Now, here are three letters I have written —one to the jewellers, this one to the portmanteau people, and this to Coutts' bank. Drive first to Coutts', give them this letter and my cheque on the British Linen Com-

C

pany. They will open an account with you, small as the sum is, because they know me very well; they will give you a cheque book, and you can give cheques to your milliners and people—poor Beatrice, I want you to be happy." I felt horrible for a moment as he said this. It was said in such a supplicatory tone, as if he wanted to propitiate me, as if I were some evil thing he feared, and he had said it before just in the same voice, " Poor Beatrice, I want you to be happy."

How this story is lengthening out. I thought I could have told it all in three or four pages, and now look, thirty pages— and yet I want to make it as long as possible. Can you guess what I say to the old doctor who comes to see me every day? I ask him, does he know how long I will live? and he shakes his head and says something about "the hands of Providence." No, I answer, not the hands of Providence, but these hands—when they have finished writing what they have to write I shall die. I know it.

CHAPTER IV

INSTRUCTIONS PERFORMED

THEN Wilder opened the hall door and I saw a splendid carriage and pair drawn up, the horses champing and flinging white foam about from their mouths. Wilder came down the steps and helped me in, the tall footman shut the door, and I heard Wilder's voice saying to the coachman, " Coutts'."

Gracious ! all the things I thought of as the carriage drove into Oxford Street. It was an open landau, and I wondered that everyone did not stop to stare at me. How strange all the people that were walking seemed, just like mean things that had no business with life ; how sweet the violets smelt in my bosom.

How nice Wilder was, not a bit good looking, but so different from the men I had mostly known. He was a gentleman, one could tell that just by his easy and languid voice; and what a hold I had upon him. And this journey to the north, I had a presentiment that it was to be strange, but how could I have told how strange, how beautiful it was to be?

Then the carriage stopped at Coutts', and the tall footman opened the door and touched his hat as I got out. I gave them Wilder's letter and my cheque, and they gave me in return a cheque book.

The next place we stopped at was the Bond Street jewellers. These are the rings I bought, see, they are on my fingers now. I never cared for diamonds. I love colour. My rings are mostly half hoops of sapphires, emeralds, and rubies; they would be vulgar only they are so glorious, and then my hands are so beautiful that you scarcely notice the rings: that was what Geraldine said. Good God! these tears will choke me: if I could only cry, but I can't, it all comes at the back of my throat, like a dull, heavy pain.

Then we drove to the other shop in Bond Street, where they sell travelling bags. I chose the most expensive I could find, a hundred and ten pounds I think it was. All the bottles had heavy gold tops, and I ordered my initials to be put on them. I ordered portmanteaux as well, and the man said everything would be ready next day by six in the evening, initials and all.

It was dark when we got to Redfern's, but that did not matter, for I had no colours to choose ; funny, wasn't it, everything I got was either white or black or grey—mourning or half-mourning. I don't know that it was so funny after all, for this kind of dress suits me. I only spent two hundred pounds on dresses ; some were to be made and sent after me when I knew the address I was going to, the others were to be sent next morning to Berkeley Square. I could have died laughing at the civility of these people at Redfern's, they thought I was some great lady—and so I was.

It was eight o'clock before I got back to Berkeley Square that evening.

CHAPTER V

WE SAY GOOD-BYE

ALL the next day I spent in the house, most of the time in the room with Wilder. How that man depressed me. A great fire was lit in the library, and he sat over it with his hands on his knees and his eyes fixed on the burning coals ; the decanter of opium was standing on the mantelpiece, a wine glass beside it, and every now and then he would pour himself out a thimbleful and sip it.

That was a pleasant sight to have to sit and watch, but I didn't much care. I sat in an armchair looking at my rings and the tips of my beautiful new shoes ; it was so delightful to have all these things again ; and sometimes I would look at Wilder's rounded back and his shiny old coat, thinking how funny it was that he had given me all these things.

Sometimes I spoke to him and he always answered, speaking in a dreamy sort of voice. I found out that he was .a spiritualist, and all the pictures about the room were " spirit faces,"—that is what he called them, all except the picture with " Swedenborg " written on it.

Then, after dinner, at about nine o'clock, he said that he must take leave of me. He took me by the hand, and the whole time he was speaking he held it, wringing it now and then till I could almost have cried out with pain. This is what he said as well as I can remember—

" I must take leave of you now. I want you to start early in the morning for Yorkshire ; you will go to my country house at Ashworth,"—a long pause, and I saw the drops of sweat stand out on his forehead. " ' The Gables,' that is the name of my house. You will change at Leeds and get on a branch line ; it's only an hour's journey from Leeds."

He spoke with difficulty, and caught at his breath.

" I have telegraphed for the carriage to meet you at the station."

Another pause, then speaking like a maniac, he seized both my hands.

" I am putting in your grasp the only thing I love, I am stealing a march on Fate, boldly and desperately I commit this act, if the end is mutual love all will be right. I shall pray without ceasing till we meet again, good-bye, good-bye."

He was devouring my hands with kisses ; then he rushed from the room. I was almost sure now that he was mad, those spirit faces and that opium—oh, there could scarcely be a doubt. The thought pleased me somehow, it made me less afraid of something — something, I don't exactly know what, a kind of horror had been haunting me all day, a foreboding of strange and terrible things to come. We old families have these powers of second sight, at least the north country families have. " We old families," perhaps you

are laughing at those words from *my* mouth ;
well—laugh.

I went up to my bedroom, and there I
found the dressing bag and the portmanteaux
all standing open and waiting to be packed.
I felt just like a robber as I put my silks
and satins, bonnets and hats, boots and
shoes, in their proper places. Then I undressed and sprang into bed. I was almost
tired already of my new life, my old dreams
came back to me, would I meet someone
nice to-morrow ? Then I thought of Wilder
and his spirit faces, and his round back, and
his opium decanter, and I laughed till the
bed shook.

And yet I liked him, this Wilder, with
his strange, weary-looking face, and his
cheques and carriages and horses.

I fell asleep.

CHAPTER VI

—AND I START

I WAS wakened next morning by a knock at the door and a voice telling me that it was eight o'clock. As I jumped out of bed the very first thought that struck me was, " Shall I meet someone to-day ? " It was what I was thinking when I fell asleep.

I was dressed in an hour. All my portmanteaux were packed, they only wanted strapping ; and I said to myself, " The butler can do that." I was not going to spoil my hands strapping them. Then I came down stairs to the breakfast room where the butler was waiting, a grave looking man of whom I had caught a glimpse last night.

When I had finished he said the carriage was in waiting, and I asked him to have my things brought down ; he said that was done already. And behold, when I reached the hall door, a carriage stood there, closed, with a basket arrangement on the top, and all my portmanteaux piled upon it. My travelling bag was inside. The footman shut the door with a snap, touched his hat again, jumped on the box, and we drove off.

I began to think whether I was a fool or not to leave Wilder. I had such a hold upon him, and now I was going I didn't know where. His country house, " The Gables," that sounded very fine, but for all that, I felt nervous at going off like this, away up to the north of England—to do what ?

But it was too late to turn back now, for the carriage was entering St Pancras station.

CHAPTER VII

NORTH !

THE footman got all my luggage together, and bought me a first-class ticket, and whilst he was getting me the ticket I went into the refreshment room and bought half a dozen packets of cigarettes and a little box of matches ; smoking soothes my nerves.

Then I walked to the B platform, if I remember right, where the Leeds express was standing, the footman following with my dressing bag. Gracious ! how civil the guard was : he made me get into a saloon carriage, and called me "my lady," and told me I could have a luncheon basket or tea if I liked, he would telegraph on to Normanton about it. I began wondering, was it my face or the footman that made him so civil, perhaps it was both—heigh-ho.

44

I write a fearful hand. I was never intended for an author. I'm so lazy and so
weak just now, that it's almost too much
trouble to dip the pen in the ink pot; how-
ever, on I must go.

There was a great fat man and a great
fat woman in the saloon carriage, immensely
rich, I suppose—cotton spinners or something of that sort. How these idiots stared
at me out of the corners of their eyes; they
had heard the old guard calling me "my
lady." They would have licked my boots,
those people would. I spoke to them, asked
them did they object to smoking, and they
said "no," both together, so I lit a cigarette.
That made them certain I was a duchess.
They got out at Normanton, and the guard
brought me a luncheon basket, and a little
tea tray, teapot and all, which he said I
could take on in the carriage to Leeds; so I
had luncheon, and then I had tea, and then
I smoked cigarettes and dreamed, whilst
the train whirled away north, north, north.
Oh this north, why did I ever come
here ?

It was late in the day when we reached Leeds, the air was chill ; it was like finding oneself in a new world. Women were standing about the platform with their heads covered with shawls ; they had clogs on their feet, and one could hear them go click, clack. I gave the old guard a sovereign. I felt sorry to part with him, he seemed the last thing connecting me with the south. I felt like a lost dog. I had never felt so all that horrible time in London : that is strange, is not it? Now, when I was rich and bowed down to, I felt like a lost dog.

I had to wait two hours for the branch train, and as it left Leeds I looked out of the window. It was a vile place, all manufactories, long chimneys, furnaces, smoke.

Then, after a bit, I saw the country, all hills and twilight, dark stone walls, desolate-looking fields, and then—a shiver ran through me—I had seen this country before. Where? Never in this life. It was the first time I had ever been north.

We stopped at little tiny stations, and I felt tired as death when at last we drew up at a station with " Ashworth " on the lamps.

I put my head out of the window, and I saw a tall footman standing on the platform amongst a lot of porters, and country women with their heads covered with shawls. I beckoned to him, and he came at a run.

" Are you Mr Wilder's footman ? "

" Yes, ma'am."

" Oh, just see to my luggage, please," I said, getting out. I followed him to the road beside the station where a carriage was waiting, a closed carriage and pair, just like the one that had driven me to the station in London.

We passed four desolate-looking cross-roads. The moon, which had risen, was lighting all the scenery round about, and I pulled down the left-hand window to get a glimpse of the view and a breath of the keen, pure air.

On a hill opposite I saw the ruins of a castle cut sharp against the sky. I had

seen that castle before. Was I positive?
Positive. Look! I said to myself. Look
at that white zig-zag pathway down the
hill, look at the hill itself. Then, as I
looked, an indescribable feeling came over
me, a delightful, far-away sort of feeling.
It seemed dawn, bright, clear, and cold.
I thought I could catch the sound of a
distant horn, I thought I could feel the
claws of a falcon on my wrist. I seemed
riding on a horse, not as a woman rides,
but as a man. I felt unutterably happy.
It was the happiness of love. You understand me, I was perfectly well awake, but
this feeling, how can I describe it, so dim,
sweet, and far-away.

Then the carriage stopped. It seems
that I had put my finger through the little
ivory ring of the check-string, and had
pulled it without knowing. The footman
came to the window, and touched his hat.

"Can you tell me the name of that
castle?" I asked. "That castle on the
hill."

"Castle Sinclair, ma'am."

"Oh! drive on, please." I think I said "Drive on, please," but I cannot be sure; at all events we drove on. I was not terrified, I was dazed.

Then, through the rumbling of the carriage wheels I thought I could again catch the sound of the distant horn. I tried—how I tried—to catch the feeling of early dawn, to feel again the tiny claws of the falcon upon my wrist.

What hunting morning was that, so dim and far away? To where was I riding? With whom was I in love? And I was a man then, so it seemed to me.

D

CHAPTER VIII

THE DIMLY-PAINTED FACE

AT last we stopped at a lodge. I heard someone cry " Gate," a creaking noise, and then we bowled smoothly up a long avenue thick-set with trees.

We stopped before a huge portico. Oh, that portico set with pillars. I almost sobbed. Was it to here that I had been riding with the falcon on my wrist? Look at the dull grey stone, the fluted pillars, the great oak door. Then the oaken door opened wide, a rush of lamplight filled the portico, and I saw an old butler with white hair waiting for me. As I entered the great hall set round with armour and galleries, the old butler bowed before me—he looked scared.

I did not notice him. How could I notice anything? An ordinary woman might have shrieked aloud, but I — I neither shrieked nor swooned.

I remember trying to take my gloves off, then I gave up the attempt, and followed a maid-servant up the broad staircase I knew so well, along the passage I knew so well, into a bedroom that had once been mine. I suppose you will think I am telling lies. Well, you can think so if you like, but people don't tell lies just for fun when they have a churchyard cough like mine, spitting blood every now and then, and knowing that every spot of blood is a seal on their death-warrant.

I took off my bonnet and travelling cloak, looked at myself in the cheval glass, and then came down stairs.

Supper was laid for me in the dining-room; *this* room I did not know, not a bit. Perhaps, after all, thought I, the whole thing is a mistake, a fancy. If I had been here before I ought to recognise the dining-room of all rooms. Then a

thought struck me, and I asked the maid
servant who was waiting—

" Has this room always formed part of
the house ; I mean, has it always been used
as a dining-room ? "

" Oh no, ma'am, it was built by Mr
Arthur."

" Added on to the house ? "

" Yes, ma'am."

That sounded queer, didn't it ?

" How long ago was it built ? "

" About sixty years I believe, ma'am."

Sixty years, oh, I was riding with that
falcon on my wrist ages before that. Do
you know that the fact of my *not* recognis-
ing this room impressed me more than
the fact of my having recognised all the
other things ?

After supper I was sitting at the table
thinking, when I heard someone softly
entering the room behind me. I turned
and saw the butler with white hair ; he
held a book in his hand.

" Please, ma'am, Mr Wilder asked me to
give you this."

"Mr Wilder?"

"Yes, ma'am, he wrote from London."

"Thanks."

I took the book; it was bound in red morocco, and on the cover was written in gold letters the word "Pictures." Pictures, a book of pictures, just as if I were a little girl wanting amusement! Then I opened it and saw that it was only a catalogue of pictures.

Here were the dining-room pictures.

"Gerard Dow, Portrait of himself. Poussin, Nymphs bathing, &c., &c."

Here was the gallery.

"Wilder, Wilder," nothing but Wilders.

"Sir Geoffry Wilder, justice of appeal, in his robes." Stay. Here was something round which a red pencil mark had been drawn, "Portrait of Gerald Wilder and Beatrice Sinclair, No. 112."

Beatrice Sinclair—that was *I*. I felt trembling with excitement, all the strangeness of the last three days had got into a focus. This picture of which the name was drawn round with red was what Wilder had sent me down to see. I was going to see my own portrait, of that I felt certain. But stay, there was something more to be read.

"Gerald Wilder slew Beatrice Sinclair in a fit of passion. Why, it was never discovered. They were engaged to be married. He destroyed himself with the poisoned wine which he had given to her, drinking it from the same cup."

This was written in Wilder's scraggy hand-writing.

"Ha!" thought I, "so Gerald Wilder slew me in some past life; well, I don't bear him any grudge, he must have been a horribly wicked man though, for all that. Now, I'll ring for the butler to show me this picture."

I rang, and the old fellow came.

"Get a lamp, please. I wish to look at the picture gallery."

"The picture gallery, ma'am."

"Yes."

"It's very dark, ma'am, at this hour. Hadn't you better wait till morning?"

" No, I wish to go now."

" Very well, ma'am."

He shuffled out, and returned in a minute or so with a lamp. Then I followed him.

As he opened the oak door of the picture gallery the lamp light rushed in before us, and I saw two long walls covered with the stern faces of the dead and gone Wilders; dim and faint they all looked in the faint light, just like ghosts. We walked down the centre of the gallery. I was looking for my face amongst all these strangers, but I could not find it.

I touched the old man on the arm, " Which is the picture of Beatrice Sinclair ? " He made no reply, but the lamp in his hand shook with a noise like the chattering of teeth. Then he walked to a picture set in a black ebony frame.

" This is it," he said, " see."

I noticed that he did not say ma'am, but I did not notice it much, I was so engaged with the face of this Beatrice.

At first I felt pleased, then disappointed.

She was very pretty, but not in the *least* like *me*. Then, as I looked, I could scarcely believe my eyes. A dimly-painted face began to grow out of the background—a man's face, with long flowing hair ; his eyes were turned towards Beatrice, they seemed also turned towards me. It was myself. This man's portrait was *my* portrait, the face larger and more masculine, but the same.

Then the old butler dropped the lamp, and it smashed to pieces on the floor. I thought I could hear him weeping in the darkness, but I am not sure. I felt I was in the room with a ghost, and I remember catching the old man's arm, and his leading me towards the light glimmering in from the hall.

CHAPTER IX

GERALDINE

" WELL, suppose I was once a man, suppose I was Gerald Wilder," I said to myself as I went into the library and music room, where a fire was lit, " Oh, bosh—and yet——"

I shut the library door and looked round. Thousands of books, a grand piano standing open, cigar boxes, cigarette boxes, easy chairs, turkey carpet. I lit a cigarette, and turned to the piano. I play well, but I am always too weak to play now. Here was Schuman, Chopin, everything in a classical way.

I like Chopin.

As I played I sometimes stopped to think and knock the ashes from my cigarette. The wind had risen and was blowing in gusts

—oh that wind of autumn, how melancholy it sounds.

As I was playing I caught the sounds of horses' feet, then the crash of wheels upon gravel. It stopped, a carriage had drawn up at the hall door, " Could it be Wilder ? "

I listened. Someone was let in. I heard the sound of voices, then everything was still. I rose from the piano and went to the door. I opened the door softly about an inch, and peeped through the crack. I saw a girl, but, as her back was towards me, I could not see her face. She was un-winding herself from a huge cloak of furs. The sallow-faced housemaid was standing waiting—I suppose for the cloak. Then I closed the door as softly as I had opened it, and sat down in one of the armchairs by the fire. I felt excited, why, I could not tell.

I was staring into the fire point blank, just as an owl stares at the sun, but I did not see the fire, I could only see the long slit-like picture, the strip of shining oak floor, the figure of the girl with her head thrown back, and her body, with its snake-like movement, winding free of the cloak.

Who was she? this girl. She had come in that carriage. She had been let in out of the autumn night. I had seen her taking off her cloak. I knew nothing more about her, so why—why did my heart become all of a sudden so fussy and fluttering like a bird disturbed in its nest, why—ah, it seemed to me that with her had been let in the far-off sound of that ghostly horn, with her had been let in the unseen falcon whose claws were now again resting upon my wrist—moving, moving, as the body they supported balanced itself uneasily, tightening now as the balance was nearly lost, loosening now as it was regained.

I sat listening. Not a sound. These great oak doors were so thick that a person might walk about in the hall and not be heard in the library. The clock on the mantel gave the little hiccup it always makes at five minutes to the hour; I looked up at the dial, it pointed to five minutes to nine.

Then a knock came to the door.   I started
and turned round.   It was only the old
butler.   I felt just as if a bucket of luke-
warm water had been emptied on me,—
deep disappointment, why I felt so I can't
tell.   He wanted to know if I required
anything more to eat—supper.

No, I required nothing to eat.

He stood shuffling at the door as if he
wanted to say something, his dismal old
face looked more troubled than ever.   I
thought for a moment he was going to
cry.   Then suddenly he shut the door and
came across the room.   He stood before
me, twiddling a book that lay on a little
table.   He looked at the carpet, then at the
fire, then at me, then he spoke—

" I have been in the service of the family
forty and nine years, ma'am."

" Have you? " I answered, I didn't know
what else to say.

" Forty and nine years come next October.
Oh, ma'am, I've seen strange things in
those years, and—the world's a strange
place."

" It is."

" Ma'am, Miss Geraldine knows you are here, and she will come in to see you presently."

" Miss Geraldine—was — was that the young lady—I mean, was it she who arrived in the carriage just now ? "

" It was, ma'am, and that's why I want to tell you. Mr James told me to tell you ; it's only beknownst to Mr James and I—God help me—God help us all—Miss Geraldine —is a boy."

" A boy," I said, half rising out of my chair ; " what do you say—how—how can a girl be a boy ? "

" Hush, ma'am, for the love of God don't speak above your breath. People may be listening, and no one knows it, *not even Miss Geraldine herself.*"

I was sitting now with my mouth hanging open like a trap ; I must have looked the picture of a fool.

" Not even herself, God bless her sweet face, not even herself, and that's not the worst, ma'am,—she *is* a girl, though she's been born a boy."

The old fellow had suddenly collapsed into the easy chair opposite to me ; he had taken his face between his scraggy old hands, his head was bent between his knees, the light of the lamp fell on the shiny black back of his coat. I shall never forget him as he sat there, speaking between his legs as if to someone under the chair.

" She's Beatrice Sinclair, that's who she is, and they must be blind who don't see it. Beatrice Sinclair, Beatrice Sinclair, she, the one that was killed long and ages ago by Sir Gerald. Beatrice Sinclair, whose picture is in the gallery, and that's who she is, that's who she is."

He was rocking about and droning this out like a dirge. I can tell you I felt shivering and fascinated. Then all at once he sat up and seemed to remember himself. I saw tears on his poor old face. He seemed trying to rise out of the arm chair.

" Sit down, don't get up," I said. " Tell me, for I must know, tell me exactly what you know, tell me all about it, and how it is that Miss Geraldine is—what she is."

"It was done to avoid the evil chance, ma'am."

"What do you mean?"

"You must know, ma'am, that the two houses of Sinclair and Wilder——"

"Yes, I think I know what you are going to say; you mean that the Sinclairs have always killed the eldest sons of the Wilders, —it's a kind of fate. Mr James Wilder told me all about it."

"Yes, mam, that's it. Well, when this child was born Mrs Wilder only survived the birth some two hours, and Mr James, almost mad with grief at her death, seemed like a thing gone silly; then, after some weeks, he quieted down, and all the love he had for his wife seemed to settle on this his only child. It was a boy, and that, mam, was the trouble; if it had been a girl! but no, it was a boy, and the eldest and only boy, and doomed, that was Mr James' word, I've heard him speaking it to himself as he has stood looking out of the window at the park, the one word, 'doomed—doomed.' He took me into his confidence, he said to me once,

"The Sinclairs ride through my dreams,
their ghosts are round me, but they shall
not have my child." He would have gone
mad, I do believe he would, only that he
thought of a plan. He took me into his
confidence, and between us we did it. The
child's name was changed from Gerald to
Geraldine, and the child was brought up
as a girl. No one in the house knew; all
the servants were dismissed but me, 'We
are safe now,' said Mr James. Ma'am,
do you know that from the lodge
gates this park is surrounded by a stone
wall, sixteen miles long and six feet high?
it cost a mine of money, but it was built.
Do you know that Miss Geraldine has
never been beyond that wall? There are
sixty and more miles of drives all through
the park, and there the horses that draw
her carriage can go at a gallop and go all
day without crossing the same ground twice
over. There are lakes, and fountains, and
imitation rivers, and that's the world she's
only known. It cost two hundred thousand
pounds a-doing, but it was done. Well,

ma'am, things went like a marriage bell till
Miss Geraldine was past fourteen ; then one
day Mr James came out of the picture gallery
with his face like a ghost, and he caught
me by the arm so that I thought I'd have
screeched with the pain of it, and he says,
' James, James, the Sinclairs have got us.'
Those were his very words, and with that he
led me into the gallery, right to the ebony
frame with Mr Gerald's picture and the
picture of Beatrice Sinclair, and there, sure
enough, was the likeness. Miss Geraldine
had grown the living image of Miss Beatrice
Sinclair ; we hadn't noticed the likeness
before, but it was there, sure and sorrowful.

"After that Mr James fell away, like.
He took to the opium, and took to it awful.
He followed Miss Geraldine like a dog. He
had it in his head that *he* was doomed to
kill her, till, it was three years ago now,
ma'am, Mr James, who had taken to spiritual-
ism, got a message saying that the last of
the Sinclairs was alive and doomed to kill
the last of the Wilders, that the only chance

was to bring them together and leave them to fate.

"Then Mr James began to search for this —this last of the Sinclairs. He searched the world, that he did; his agents went to all foreign parts, to India and everywhere, till a few days ago, and I got telegram after telegram from him to prepare the house, that he had found the person he wanted. Oh, I was glad, that I was, when I saw you, ma'am, I nearly fell on the ground."

"You think I am like Mr Gerald?"

The old fellow made no answer for a moment, then he got up off his chair to go.

"Ma'am, you'll excuse my sitting in your presence, you'll excuse my talking so free, but I am old, and I have grown to love that child as if it was my own, it's that sweet and that innocent, and, saving your presence, ma'am, doesn't know what a man is, or a woman is neither. I've heard talk of angels, but there never was an angel more innocent, no, nor more sweet; and to think of harm coming to it, it that is so unharmful. It wrings my heart, the thought of it do;

many's the night, ma'am, I've woke in a sweat thinking I've heard the trumpeter, but it's been only ringing in my ears——".

"The trumpeter, what do you mean?" I asked.

"The ghost, ma'am, Sir—Sir Gerald's ghost, it comes through the passages at midnight blowing a trumpet always before the eldest son is killed. Oh, ma'am, it's a fearful sound and a fearful sight."

"When was it heard last?"

"Twenty-three years ago, ma'am, the night before Mr Reginald was killed by Mr Wilfred Sinclair."

Twenty-three years, that was exactly my age.

"It has not been heard since, not even at Mrs Wilder's death?"

"No, ma'am, that trumpet never sounds for the death of women, not for no one, only the eldest son who is about to die."

"Did anyone hear or see this trumpeter the last time he came?"

"I did, ma'am, see him, and hear him both."

"Tell me about it. Did you see his face?"

"No, ma'am." Somehow I knew the old fellow was telling a lie, and that he *had* seen the trumpeter's face, but I said nothing.

"No, ma'am, not distinctly so to say. I was a young servant then, an under-butler, and in the night, when I was sound asleep, I suddenly woke and sat up to listen. The house was as still as death, and there was nothing to hear, yet I sat listening and listening and straining my ears, waiting to hear something that I knew would come. Oh, ma'am, I needn't have strained my ears, for suddenly the most *awful* blast of a trumpet shook the house, I sickened, and thought I'd have died, for though I knew nothing of the ghost, or the history of the house, I knew that the sound of that trumpet was not right; it stopped for a moment after the first blast, and then it came again, louder and louder. I rushed out of my room into the dark passage, then, ma'am, I ran down the passage and down the servants' staircase until I found the first floor. I ran down the corridor till I came to the great staircase overlooking the hall, and there I saw him. There was no light, but I saw him, for there was light all round him. He was crossing the great hall when I caught a glimpse of him. His long black hair was tossed back, and he had to his mouth a great, glittering, silvern trumpet, and I could see his cheeks puffed out as he blew. He was dressed like the portrait of Sir Gerald."

"You think it was Sir Gerald's ghost?"

"Yes, ma'am, he has been recognised over and over again."

"Did anyone else hear him?"

"No, ma'am, only me. I told the master about it next day. No one had heard it but me. Then the message came to say Mr Reginald was dead."

I sat silent for a moment, listening to the wind as it sighed outside, then I said—

"Do you expect to hear the trumpeter again?"

"No, ma'am, not since you've come."

"How is that?"

The old fellow hung his head.

"Come now," I said; "tell me this. Don't you think you see the ghost in the flesh? I am exactly twenty-three, and it is twenty-three years since the trumpeter has been. Do you not think that my coming is the return of the trumpeter— without the trumpet?"

I shall never forget the old man's face as I said this; it absolutely became glorified with—what—I don't know, perhaps hope.

"Oh, ma'am," said he, "I did see the trumpeter's face, despite the lie I told you; it was your face, line for line. But you will never hurt the child, that I know, for the good God has sent you into the flesh, and it's as much as if He had said the trumpet shall never be heard again, which is saying the eldest son will never be killed again by the Sinclairs."

Then the old fellow left the room and shut the door.

And I sat brooding over the fire, half-pleased, half-frightened, half-dazed. The old butler's manner all through his conversation had been just like James Wilder's in London. They both seemed to consider me as something to be feared and propitiated.

And this Geraldine, this extraordinary being whose fate seemed wound up in mine, why should they fear any hurt to this Geraldine from me? I could not hurt a fly, much less this creature whom I had begun to like instinctively already.

Did anyone ever hear of such a thing as to bring up a boy as a girl? Only that weird looking James Wilder, with his round back and his opium decanter, could have thought of such a thing; she—he—she, what shall I call him or her? She was going to pay me a visit to-night; when would she come? What was she doing now? at supper perhaps, what was she having for supper?

A tap at the door.

The handle turned, and the door opened.

CHAPTER X

AND this was Geraldine Wilder, or Gerald
—Geraldine Wilder, if you please.

This half ghostly being, with brown rippling
hair and a face like the face of a wild rose.
And the dress of wonderful black lace that
seemed draped round the slight figure by
the fingers of the wind, and the milk white
neck, rising like the stem of some graceful
flower to support the small brown head, and
the *elegance* of the whole apparition. I love
to think of it even still. But it was Beatrice
Sinclair. Oh, yes, beyond any manner of
doubt, it was Beatrice Sinclair, and as we
gazed at each other for one short second
the claws of the falcon *tore* at my
wrist.

Then this vision of the past came across

72

the room and held up its face to be kissed. And it was like two dead lovers kissing through a veil—so it seemed to me. And yet I could have laughed as she sat down in the great arm chair opposite mine, to see the subtle turn of the body with which she arranged the train of her dress, the graceful manner of sitting down, and then to remember that " Miss Geraldine was a boy ; " and then the glimpse of immaculate white petticoat ! it semed like a witticism one could not laugh at because one was in church.

I laugh now as I think of it, at least I smile, for I haven't strength to get up a real laugh, and then somehow I cry, perhaps because I am so weak.

Geraldine sat down, and then we began to talk. I talked at random, for I was so busy examining and admiring her I couldn't think of other things. The little division at the end of the nose seemed somehow the most delightful thing I had ever seen, except maybe the arched instep of the tiny foot that peeped like a brown mouse from beneath the skirt.

What a lout I felt beside her. I felt awkward, and stupid, and just as a mole might feel if it were made to sit in the sun. I began to stutter and stammer, and might have made a dreadful fool of myself, only that the recollection shot up in my mind, " she's a boy " ; as long as I kept that in mind I was all right, but the instant I began to think of her as a girl, my stupidity returned.

We talked, mercy, what modest and inno-cent talk, the whole college of Cardinals and the old Pope himself might have listened and been the better for it, but they would not have been much the wiser.

" Gerald—I mean Geraldine—how old are you ? "

" I am sixteen years."

" You have never been away from home, you have never seen a city ? "

" What is a city ? "

" Oh, it's a place, a horrible place where it's all smoke, and houses, and noise."

Geraldine shook her head. She could not imagine what such a place as this could be like.

"Are there many more people in the world from where you come?" asked Geraldine after a pause, resting her chin on her hand and gazing at me with a deep, far-away look, as if she recognised me dimly but was not quite sure.

"Oh, yes ; but has your father never told you about the world and the people in it?"

"No," said Geraldine, with a shake of the head; "he told me it was a bad place, and I must never go there, that was all."

"Have you never wished to go there?"

"No, never, till—till now."

"Why now?"

"I would like to go there if it is the place you come from."

Geraldine was gazing at me now intensely —I know no other word—with eyes that seemed appealing to me to say something; never had I been gazed at so before.

I could only falter out, "Why?"

"Because," said Geraldine, "I think I

know where you come from, I think I have seen you there, but it was in a dream, and we were not dressed as we are, but I am not sure. *Who* are you?"

I have never heard anything so soft and yet so full of a kind of fire as those words.

"Has not your father told you, Geraldine?"

"No—he said a lady was coming to see me, but that was all."

"I am Beatrice Sinclair, Geraldine."

"But that is only a name."

A thought shot like a horrible zig-zag firework through my brain; it was, "Geraldine, I was once your murderer."

Then bang from tragedy to comedy. I began to laugh, for no earthly reason, and Geraldine caught the laugh as it flew on her beautiful lips, and we both laughed at each other like two children—at nothing. Then we talked for an hour about—nothing.

As Geraldine vanished that night to her own rooms I called her back, and she came back from the dark corridor like a beautiful ghost.

I only wanted to kiss her again, but she

seemed to think that a perfectly good reason for my calling her back.

Then I went to bed and cried like a fool ; then I got out of bed and hunted round the room in the dark, guess what for—a match-box, guess what to find—my cigarette box. I really think I must once have been a man.

CHAPTER XI

THE LITTLE BLACK BOOK

I FOUND it, and having lit the candle by my bedside I got back into bed and began to smoke. The fumes of the tobacco, the utter silence of the house broken only by the occasional sighing of the wind in the trees outside, the exquisite room in which I was lying with its painted ceiling and rose petal coloured hangings, the image of Geraldine, all combined to produce in my mind a sort of delicious intoxication.

I saw now vaguely the wonderful dream that was beginning to unfold around me, the fairy tale of which I was to be the hero. I saw once more the face that had come back from the dark corridor to be kissed —ah me !

My hands rested upon a little black

covered book, I had found it upon the mantelpiece, and had taken it into bed with me, thinking to put my cigarette ashes upon it. Instead of that I had shaken them off, without thinking, upon the floor.

I opened it. The first thing I saw was the picture of a skull drawn in faded ink upon the yellow title-page. Then, under the skull, written in what, even in those old days, must have been a boy's scrawl, this—

" The blacke worke of deathe herein sette downe is bye yᵉ hande of Geoffry Lely hys page."

Whose page? I knew well.

Then, on the next leaf, in the same handwriting, but smaller and more cramped, I read the following. It was written in the old English style, and the queer spelling of the words I cannot imitate, as I write only from remembrance.

" Before daylight of that dark and bloody day a week agone now, by lantern light we left the court-yard and rode down the avenue, Sir Gerald on his black horse Badminton, I on the bay mare Pimpernel. In the black dark of the avenue nothing could I see, but followed, led by the sound of Badminton's hoofs, the clink of Sir Gerald's scabbard, and the tinkling bells of the little hawke that sat hooded and drowsing upon his wrist.

" Had I followed a common man I might have asked of him what place hath a hawke on the wrist of a man with a sword by his side and pistols at his holster, but Sir Gerald I have followed my life long without question, and without question would have ridden behind him to death.

" In the road beyond the darkness of the trees we paused, each at five paces from the other ; the clouds in the easternmost part of the sky were all cracked where the day was breaking through ; a dour and dark morning was it, and no sound to hear but a plover crying weep, weep, and the little tinkle ever and anon of the hawke's bells.

"I watched the wind toss Sir Gerald's black hair and lift the plume of his hat, and let it fall, and lift it again, and let it fall, light as if 'twere the fingers of a woman at play with it. He was resting in his saddle as if a-thinking, then touching Badminton with the spur, he led the way from the road on to the moor, the two horses' hoofs striking as one.

"We passed the shoulder of the hill and down to the Gimmer side, and there by the river we stopped again and Sir Gerald sat and seemed a-listening to the mutter of the water and the wuther of the wind in the reeds ; but he was in sore trouble, that I knew by the way his head was bent and by the sighs that broke from him ever and anon.

"And where his trouble lay I knew, for I had but to look the way his head was turned, and see Castle Sinclair, all towers and turrets, set up against the morning

F

which was breaking quickly out from under the clouds.

" As we sat I heard a horn sounding beyond the river bank and the yelp of a hound blown on the wind thin and sharp, and in the distance, crossing the ford of the Gimmer, I saw three horsemen ; they were Sinclairs, that I knew,—General James Sinclair rode first, I could tell him by the great size of himself and his horse, and of the other two I knew one to be Rupert and the other George, but which was which no eye of mortal could tell in the dim light that was then.

" They passed the ford and rode away, a huntsman following close on, seeming to move in the midst of a waving furze bush, which was the hounds in full pack, and the last of them we heard was the toot of the horn sounding over the hillside.

" Then Sir Gerald touched Badminton again with spur, and we rode along the river bank to the ford, still warm from the crossing of the Sinclairs ; and the ford behind us, we set our horses' heads straight for Castle Sinclair.

" The morning was up now, and we could hear the cocks a-crowing from the barnes lying to the thither side of the castle. In the courtyard we drew bridle, and Sir Gerald dismounted and threw his reins to me.

" At the open door above the stone steps stood Mistress Beatrice Sinclair herself ; she held in her hand a silver stirrup cup. Without doubt she had lingered at the door from seeing the huntsmen off to their hunt, held mayhap by the fineness of the morning.

" I saw Sir Gerald advance to her, his plumed hat in hand, and they passed into the great hall so that I could not see them more, and there I sat to wait with no sound to save me from the stillness but the cawing of the rooks in the elm tops below, and the grinding of Badminton's teeth as they chawed on the bit.

" The clock in the turret struck six, and I sat a-thinking of Mistress Beatrice Sinclair, holding her beautiful face up to the eye of my mind, and putting beside it for contrast the dark face of Sir Gerald. Then the clock struck seven and Badminton he struck with his hind hoof on the yard pavement and neighed as if calling after his master.

"Then five minutes might have gone. I saw Sir Gerald's figure at the door, his face white as the ashes of wood, and he stumbling like a man far gone in drunkness. But drunkness it was none and that I knew, but some calamity dire and fell, and I put Badminton up to the steps in a trice, for I read the look in Sir Gerald's black eye which meant ' flight.'

" As he rose into the saddle a window shot open above, and a woman's voice cried, ' Stop them, stop them, my lady is dead, he has killed her ! ' Then, reeling in my saddle with the horror of the thing, I put the bridle rein to Sir Gerald's hands. He heard and saw nothing, that I knew by his eyes and his face, so, leaving Pimpernel to care for herself, I sprang on Badminton behind

Sir Gerald, and taking the reins with my hands stretched out, I put spurs deep into his sides.

"The wind rushed in my ears and the cries of the woman grew faint ; down hill we tore, I heard the splashing of the Gimmer water round Badminton's legs and the hoofs of him rattling on the pebbles of the ford. Then I heard behind me the clashing of the alarum bell of the castle.

"Something in Sir Gerald's right hand, hanging loose, took my eye, and I sickened at the sight, for it was the body of the little brown hawk crushed to death.

"I looked back, Castle Sinclair stood out against the blood red of the sky. Up suddenly against us rose a great man on a black horse. It was General James Sinclair spurring for the castle ; he threw his horse on his haunches. Badminton he reared, and Sir Gerald fell forward before me on his neck, his dark hair all mixed with the mane. Then I drew rein, I called to Sir Gerald, but no answer made he ; his lips were blue, dead he was as the little hawk crushed in his hand, dead as Mistress Beatrice Sinclair, poisoned with the selfsame poison he always carried in his ring ; dead as I Geoffry Lely shall be, and that soon, from the sorrow that has fallen on me since that dark and bloody day."

There the writing stopped. I only quote from memory, but it is a good memory, for that strange bit of writing burnt itself deeply into my heart. It occupied six pages. The seventh was covered by Wilder's handwriting. It was the beginning of a horrible list, the list of the eldest sons of the Wilders. Each name stood there bracketed with the name of a Sinclair. I knew what that meant. This was the way :—

Beatrice Sinclair—Gerald Wilder.
John Wilder—Rupert Sinclair.
Adam Wilder—James Sinclair-Sinclair.
Athelstan Wilder — Arthur Reginald
Sinclair,

and so on.

That list horrified me, I could not go on

with it. At the foot of all these names so strangely coupled together James Wilder had written a sort of prayer.

"Oh, God! how long! how much longer shall this blood red hand be held over us? I have but one little child, I implore your mercy for it. Have pity upon me and it, *we* have done no wrong."

That made my eyes swim so that I could scarcely see. I shut the little black book; it looked like a witch, and I determined to burn it. The fire was still red in the grate, so I got up and put it on the live coals. It burned quite cheerfully. I watched it as I lay in bed, and I muttered to myself, "Let the past die like that." I watched the cover all curling up, and little jets of blue flame spouting from the leather binding. Oh, if it were only as easy to burn the past as it is to burn a book! Then nothing was left but sullen-looking grey ashes, with little red points running over them.

Then I blew out my candle, and the room was in darkness. The wind sighed

outside in the tree tops.   I saw all kinds
of pictures painted on the darkness, faces,
and one angelic face, the last before I went
to sleep—Geraldine's.

CHAPTER XII

THE MORNING

A WEEK ago . had been living in——
Crescent, living in a room with an old faded
carpet on the floor, with one picture on the
walls,—and such a picture, I can see it still,
it was a German oleograph representing the
Day of Judgment, and so badly done that the
long trumpets seemed sticking in the sides
of the angels' cheeks, not out of their mouths,
and some of the devils, I remember, had their
tails growing from the middle of their backs.
The looking-glass made one look horrible,
and the handles were off the chest of drawers,
so one had to pull the drawers out with
a crooked hairpin.

I minded the picture more than anything.
Some girls would have grumbled at the chest
of drawers, and never thought of the picture,

but I have always loved beautiful things, so I suppose that is the reason why I grumbled so much at the picture and so little at the other thing.

You may think, then, how delightful it was next morning when I woke and saw the light filtering in through the rose-coloured blinds. I sat up in the bed and saw the glimmer of the great ivory hair brushes on the dressing-table. I saw my rings lying in a heap—I would never have had those rings only for Geraldine, I would never have been here, only for Geraldine, I might have been in the Thames, floating with dead cats and dogs by this, only for Geraldine. Then I fell back on the pillows, smothered with a strange kind of horror ; it was strange, because it had no reason for being. It passed away slowly like a mist dissolving, and I lay looking up at the blue ceiling, with rosy clouds painted on it, and little Cupids peeping at each other from behind them. I pulled up the blinds of my window to look out; then I opened the sash.

It was an autumn morning, warm and dark, the wind of the night before had blown half dead leaves about the garden on which my window looked; it had rained in the night, and the air was full of the smell of dampness and decay, and a faint perfume like the bitter perfume of chrysanthemums; there was just enough wind to make the trees move their leaves about, and make a noise as if they were sighing. I love this autumn weather; I don't know why, perhaps it's just because I don't know why that I love it. That seems rubbish, but I am too lazy to scratch it out. It is just like autumn now as I sit writing this, though it is early spring, and the trees are all covered with little green buds, making ready for another autumn that I shall never see.

Then I dressed. I put on three dresses, one after another, and they all seemed not good enough; but I had no more fit for morning wear, so I left on the third.

Then I came down to breakfast, and I found only one place laid. I could have broken my plate over the old butler's head,

but I didn't, and I can't for the life of me
tell why I could have done it, or why I
didn't do it. Breakfast proceeded in solemn
silence.

"Would I have ham?"

No, I would not have ham! where was
Geraldine?

Miss Geraldine breakfasted an hour ago
alone in her wing of the house; Miss
Geraldine sent her compliments, and wanted
to know if I would visit her in her own
rooms after I had finished breakfast.

He might take Miss Geraldine my compliments, and say that I would have much
pleasure in doing so. He had better go
at once. No, I required no more coffee.

He went.

Her compliments, indeed, and her wing of
the house, I wonder why she didn't send her
card. Yes, I would visit her just as often
as I pleased—yet I would not if my visits
didn't please. No, in that case I would
drown myself in the moat, but there was no
moat; well, in the big bath upstairs. And
the way the old butler said, " Miss

Geraldine" quite calmly, though he knows Miss Geraldine is a boy; and she is a boy, and she ought to be smacked for being such a prig. But why smack her when it's not her fault? No, it's James Wilder and the old butler that require smacking, and still—and still, these two old fools between them have produced, or helped to produce, this weird child, just as she is; and in all God's earth she is the most beautiful thing, and the most strange. She is like a thing made of mist, yet she is real; she is a ghost, yet one can touch her. What is she—what is he—who am I—I don't know—I don't want to know. Ha! I felt just then the claws of the little falcon pinching my wrist.

That was the jumbling kind of stuff that ran through my head as I breakfasted; then, when I had finished, instead of going at once to find Geraldine's wing of the house, I hung about the room looking at the pictures, putting off my visit just as a person puts off a bite at a peach. At last I came.

I seemed to know the way by instinct; there was no placard with " To Geraldine " on it, but I found Geraldine for all that. I crossed the hall and passed the picture gallery scarcely looking at the door. Then I lifted a heavy corded silk curtain, and found myself in a corridor. Upon my word, I thought I was in the Arabian Nights. Each side of the corridor was panelled, and on the cream white panels were painted flowers,—it was a regular flower-garden of painting. The roof was white, with coloured windows, each made in the shape of a fan. These stained glass fans were the prettiest things in the way of windows I had ever seen—so I thought. The corridor ended in a heavy curtain like the one at the other end; two doors stood on each side of the curtain. I chose the right hand door, for I guessed it belonged to the room she was in. I was right. I knocked. A voice cried, " Come in," and in I came.

Oh, this Geraldine! I must have seen her all askew last night, for now she seemed

eight times lovelier than she was then.
Who had taught this being the art of
putting on dress? Surely not James
Wilder or the old butler. This dress she
wore was made from a fabric intended to
represent the skin of some tropical lizard,
scales of golden satin on a body-ground of
dull emerald-coloured silk. She rose from
her chair like a snake from a blanket.
James Wilder, when he rose from a chair,
always reminded me of a flail in a fit.
Yet she was his son.

We said " Good morning," but we did
not kiss. Something seemed to have come
between us ; we seemed instinctively to hold
aloof from each other. The Geraldine who
came up to me last night to be kissed, just
as a tame fawn might have done, was not
exactly the Geraldine of this morning. And
yet I liked this something that had come
between us. Kisses are just like apples ;
if you can get as many as you want they
grow tasteless, and the more you pay for
them the sweeter they seem, and they are
never so sweet as when you steal them. I

never heard of a farmer robbing his own orchard, have you?

Then this fine lady sank back into the chair from which she had arisen—it was not sitting down, it was sinking down—and with a ghostly smile resumed her work. And guess the work—tapestry. Tapestry; and she had done yards of it, when she ought to have been playing at marbles and learning to swear.

As for me, I sat down plump on a chair close by, crossed my legs, and nursed my knee with my hands. I felt inclined to whistle. Remember, I was thinking of her now as a boy in petticoats, and as long as I thought of her as that I was in my right senses, that is, my everyday senses. I felt perverse, just as I always feel, and would have liked to tease—only I wouldn't have dared—this half-absurd, wholly delightful production of old James Wilder. But when I thought of her as a girl I felt—I felt the dim remembrance of a past life, and an infinite sadness.

I looked round at the room; it looked like

the inside of a shell. Fairies seemed to
have furnished it. I never saw such exquisite things before. There were cabinets
inlaid with copper on ebony, and Venice
glass that seemed coloured with tints of the
sea. A wood fire was burning on the tiled
hearth, and a great bowl of violets stood
on a table supported by carved dragons
with jewels for eyes. The smell of the
violets made me feel faint every now and
then, but the faintness went away when I
remembered this Geraldine was a boy.
"Remember that," I kept repeating to
myself. And in the middle of the room
sat Geraldine.

The long French windows were open,
and the garden, all damp and sad-coloured,
lay outside. Great chrysanthemums, potted
out, were nodding under the marble-coloured
sky, and they all seemed nodding at
Geraldine. When a hitch came in the
thread Geraldine's under lip would pout out.
I felt now and then as if I were acting
in a play, and the chrysanthemums' faces
were the faces of the audience. Perhaps

G

they were. Anyhow, I had learnt my part very badly, so it seemed to me.

The tapestry was a great blessing; one could speak or not as one pleased, and I generally preferred—not. I fell to wondering does *she* remember anything of that hunting morning so long ago : does she remember the poison, has she forgiven the poisoner, and has God ?

Then I began to talk to her again and she answered in a low measured voice that sounded to me like a bell from the far past, yet in spite of the ghostly kind of sadness with which her voice filled me, some of her answers made me laugh.

She didn't know how to read ; that came out in the course of our scrappy conversation.

" But, *Geraldine*, why—you've never read your *Bible*, then ? "

One might have thought from my tone that I was a shocked Sunday-school superintendent, and it really did seem shocking to me that a person should never have read the Bible.

" What is my Bible? " asked Geraldine, staring at me, half-frightened at my astonishment.

" Oh, it's a book. I'll tell you about it some other time, but—but you can't know Geography. Do you know where Japan is, Geraldine, or India ? "

Geraldine's head shook. She looked dazed.

" Do you know where England is ? "

Oh, yes, she knew where England was, —this house, this garden, all away beyond there, was England—all over there.

How proudly she waved the white hand. It was patriotism pure and simple. She was proud of her park, not because it was her park, but because it was her native land. Her—his—I cannot say " his," I must always say " her ; " besides, it doesn't matter now. It will never matter again, nothing will ever matter again. What gibberish I am writing ; how those trees nod and nod their heads as if they were nodding at the little graveyard " away over there," just as the chrysanthemums were nodding that morning at Geraldine.

She didn't know her Bible and she didn't know her Geography, and she didn't know "nothing." What a lot of ignorance was stowed away in that small head; but she knew something of natural history. The tapestry work had stopped, and we were walking in the little garden where the chrysanthemums were. I pointed to a snail no the path.

"What is that, Geraldine?"

"That," said Geraldine, "is a snail."

How proud she seemed of her knowledge, and how tenderly she lifted the snail on to a leaf. The clock in the clock-turret was striking noon.

"Can you read the clock, Geraldine?"

"Oh, yes, and my watch."

A watch the size of my thumb-nail was produced. How learned she was, really a kind of professor!

We walked down an alley of cypress trees without speaking, then we stopped, for the sound of a gong came roaring from the house.

It was the luncheon gong, so said Geraldine, and I suddenly woke up from a reverie to remember that I was not in the seventeenth but the nineteenth century.

CHAPTER XIII

"YOU WERE NOT DRESSED LIKE THIS"

THE old clergyman who lives at Ashworth has just been. He comes twice a week and eats a biscuit and drinks a glass of wine, and tells me we should all think on the future life, or the life to come. He asked me what I was writing, and I said— nothing.

Well—that day I had luncheon all alone. Where that other strange being had luncheon, or whether she had luncheon at all, I don't know; I had luncheon alone, and I had chops for luncheon.

What did James Wilder mean by sending me here to be driven mad? What was driving me mad? Why, Geraldine was. I had sprung at one bound into the most fabulous world of love. I could have eaten that snail she lifted on to the leaf, just because she touched it.

The old butler was meandering round the room with a dish of vegetables in his hand.

" James," I said.

" Ma'am."

" I have fallen in love with your Miss Geraldine."

" May God be thanked, ma'am."

" James," in a coaxing voice, " I want to go out for a drive with him—I mean with her—with Miss Geraldine. Do you understand ? "   •

" Yes, ma'am, and so shall I tell the horses to be put in ? "

" Why, yes, after luncheon, that is, if Miss Geraldine likes ; do you think she would like ? "

" Ma'am," in a voice like the voice of a ghost, " Miss Geraldine has been a-speaking of you to me ; she comes to me, ma'am, to tell any little trouble that may happen like as she was a boy, which she is, may God in Heaven bless her ; and she came to me last night after you'd a-gone to bed, and she said, 'James, who is Beatrice Sinclair?' Lord, ma'am, you might ha knocked me down with your finger. 'Why,' I says, Miss Geraldine, 'she's the lady just come.' Then she says 'James,' and she held down her head and all her little face grew red, 'Will she ever go away again?' 'Why, Miss Geraldine?' said I. 'Because if she does,' said she, 'I shall die; I've been waiting for her and thinking of her for years, and if she leaves me now I shall die:' those were her words."

A bucket of vitriol emptied into a furnace those words were to me.

"The horses," I cried, rising from the table, "ring for the horses; go and tell Miss Geraldine to dress, for I am going to take her for a drive. Go." I stamped my foot, I was speaking like a man. I was suddenly intoxicated. I felt hat, boots and belt upon me; the falcon was on my wrist. I clapped my hand on my left hip and was astonished to find—no sword. That, somehow, brought me to, and I sat

down at the table again feeling shrunk
—shrunk? do you understand that word?—
shrunk like an apple that has been all
winter in the cellar—shrunk like a warrior
who wakes to find himself a woman. " She
hung down her head and all her little face
grew red," how exactly those words brought
her image before me. This little milksop.
I was sitting at the table; the old butler
had gone to order the carriage ; the light
of the autumn day came greyly through
the great double windows, a spray of
withered wistaria was tapping at one of
the panes like the hand of a ghost. Before
me, on the opposite wall, hung a convex
Venetian mirror, one of those strange
mirrors that are made so perfectly and so
truly that they reflect everything just as
it is, even the atmosphere, so that a room
reflected by them seems like a real room.
I was staring at my own reflection in
the mirror, and wondering over again at
my own likeness to the portrait of Gerald
Wilder — when — the door in the mirror
opened, a figure the size of my thumb

entered the mirror room, a figure lithe and more gorgeously clad than any cater-pillar. I knew quite well that it was only Geraldine who had opened the door behind me, and was therefore reflected in the mirror. I knew that quite well, yet I watched the mirror without moving: the little figure seemed to hold me in a spell. It came up softly behind the woman seated at the table—the woman with the face so like Gerald Wilder; it paused as if undecided. I watched.

Geraldine evidently was utterly ignorant of the mirror and its picture. Geraldine the observed imagined herself unobserved: then, like a little thief, she bent her lips to kiss the woman's hair without the woman knowing. I threw my head back and caught the kiss upon my lips, I threw my arms back and caught her round the neck; never was a thief so caught in his own trap.

Then I turned round, and let her go, and confronted her, all at the same time. And there she stood, "with her head hung down and all her little face grown red."

Love has never been described properly : all that about roses and altars is nonsense. Love is like being in a beautiful and mysterious room, and you push a curtain aside and you find a more mysterious and more beautiful room, and you see another curtain. How that comparison would shock the people who write poetry. Imagine comparing love to a suite of rooms.

I shall never forget that drive ; the horses were those Russian horses that go as if they were mad ; the air was all filled with the smell of autumn, and the earth seemed as silent as the leaden-coloured sky. The park lay all dull-coloured and damp, the great trees were standing with their leaves hanging down.

Miles and miles of park we passed through; there were sober and sad-coloured hills in the distance that seemed to watch us with a mournful air. The country had for me the aspect of fate as it lay around us, silent as a dream, the trees dropped their withered leaves, the clouds passed by, the wind blew, and clouds and wind and trees all said to me in their own language, the past, the past, the past. Once Geraldine said, " When I saw you before, so long ago, you were not dressed as you are now."

No, Geraldine, I said to myself, when you saw me before, so long ago, I was dressed as a man. But I did not answer her in words.

CHAPTER XIV

THE BALLADE OF THE FALCON

To the deep window of the library, where I am sitting now wrapped in shawls and scribbling this, I came that day after our drive to sit and think, and stare out of the double windows at the dusky garden, and wait for tea. I had taken an old book from one of the library shelves. It was " The whole art of Falconry," dedicated to his Majesty, King Charles the First, by his liege servant—I forget whom.

When I was tired with looking out of the window I turned over the leaves of the book ; they smelt of age. Between the cover and the last leaf was a manuscript, the ink faded, the paper mildewed. I spelt it out in the dusk.

It was a ballad written in a curious, old-fashioned hand. It was about a little falcon which a lady had given to her lover; he killed her in a fit of passion, and he killed the little falcon, or " the little hawke," as the ballad sometimes called it, and then he killed himself. As I read it grew sadder and sadder, it seemed to moan to me like a living thing, and my eyes became blind with tears so that I could scarcely read it in the twilight. It was all about the little falcon, but I knew that the pity was meant for the cavalier. Perhaps the writer dared not express it openly, for was not the cavalier an assassin and a suicide?

This is the last verse, as well as I remember—

> " With the little falcon prest
> To his cold and lifeless breast,
> They laid him to his rest.
> And the ballade humbly prays
> The tribute of your sighs
> For the hawke's blinde little eyes,
> —And the cavalier who lies
> By the four cross ways."

Ah! the dead hand that wrote that long

ago betrayed itself in the two last lines,

"And the cavalier who lies
By the four cross ways."

I laid it down and cried as if my heart
would break. I was crying, not for the
cavalier but for "the little hawke."

CHAPTER XV

THAT night I went up to my room early. I took pens, ink, and paper with me—why I took them I had no notion—I took them. I lit all the wax lights on the mantel, and the wax lights that stood on the dressing-table. Then I stood before the dressing-table mirror looking at myself. I can see the reflection of my face still, a pale face with dark sombre eyes, and lips that curled in a sneer. That was how Gerald Wilder looked when he was in a rage. I could see now Gerald Wilder, the assassin and the suicide. I was Gerald Wilder.

Geraldine and I were inextricably en-tangled—she in the body of a boy, I in the body of a woman. Was this my punishment for that murder and that suicide committed

112

long, long ago, this blind maze of the flesh
into which I had been led? I could do one
of two things. Leave Geraldine to-morrow
morning, never to see her again, or—stay.
If I left her she would break her heart,
and die. I would break my heart, and die.
Then perhaps we might meet, and be happy
for ever. Surely, if all those stars were suns,
and if there were worlds round them like
our world, God might give us some little
place, some tiny garden out of all His
splendour. He was rich, and owned the
whole of space, and He would give something to two ghosts who had left the world
for the love of each other. That was what
would happen if we left each other—we
would grow sick and die, but we would
meet on the other side. If we remained
together, I knew that something would
happen to separate us for ever, how I
knew this I cannot tell, perhaps it was by
instinct.

I turned from the mirror to the table,
where I had placed the writing things.
Now I knew why I had brought them up:

it seems to me that we often think when we don't know we are thinking.

I sat down, and took one of the thick sheets of paper stamped in red with

"THE GABLES,
"ASHWORTH, YORKS,"

and I wrote. This is what I wrote—

"DEAR JAMES,—I know now why you have sent me down here. I have seen your Geraldine, and I love her, but I must leave her. It will kill us both, but I have chosen to die. *Can* you not see that I am your kith and kin, that I am Gerald Wilder? You have no claim on Geraldine, for she is a Sinclair, she is the dead Beatrice returned as a Wilder. I think I see it all now, if one may see anything in such awful darkness. I know, without knowing exactly *how* I know it, that if we part we shall dream of each other till we die, and that then we shall meet never to be separated, but if we remain together some fearful thing will happen and divide us, so that we may never meet again.

If I loved your son all would be right, but it is not Gerald I love, but Geraldine—Beatrice.

I am leaving here early to-morrow morning, going, I don't know where. I shall write to you.

Signed,

GERALD WILDER."

Then I directed an envelope—

JAMES WILDER, Esq.,

No.— BERKELEY SQUARE,

LONDON.

I put the letter in. I gummed it. Then I began to search for a stamp. I felt that I must stamp it to add a kind of security to my purpose, though the post did not leave until noon on the morrow. What a search I had for that stamp. I rummaged all my dress pockets ; at last I found my purse,—there were two stamps in it.

I stamped the letter carefully. I held

it in my hands as I sat over the fire.
Then, without any apparent reason, I tore
the letter slowly up into four pieces, then
into eight. Then I placed the pieces
carefully on the burning coals in the grate.
I watched the stamp burning and thought
it was a pity to see it burn, for it was
worth a penny. I saw the d e r letters of
Wilder stand out white on a bit of the
burnt envelope.

Then I took the poker and poked at
the bits of paper ash.

I was thinking.

All my life long I have loved everything
beautiful: colours have a strange fascination
for me, you could make me sad quicker
with a colour than a story or a poem;
scents and sounds have the same effect,
the smell of violets suddenly transports me
to somewhere, I don't know where, I only
know it is elsewhere. I have heard things
in music that no one has ever heard, notes
that come up again and again as the harmony
moves to the end of its story, sombre notes
full of fate. I have seen people listening to

music and their faces had no more expression than jugs; I have heard women talking of the opera, utterly unconscious of the story the music they were listening to was telling them.

I was sitting by the fire thinking; the bits of burnt paper had flown up the chimney in a hurry, perhaps the devil had called them. I was thinking in pictures, and I felt unutterably happy and relieved now that I had written my letter to James Wilder—and burnt it.

I saw my room in —— Crescent, The creature that had inhabited that room was not *I*. I saw the room so distinctly that I saw on a shelf an old tattered book— Dumas' "Three Musketeers." I used to read it sometimes at nights, and I used to wonder how it was possible that the Duke of Buckingham could have loved Anne of Austria in the insane manner in which he did; now I saw at a glance that such love was quite possible, and no fable. He loved her because she was unattainable, she was a Queen; he could never have loved an ordinary woman like that. A soap bubble is the most beautiful thing in the world because it is so unattainable, you cannot put it in your pocket.

Then Geraldine suddenly appeared before my mind. Not only Geraldine, but the thousand and one things that made her up. I have told you before that colour and scent and sound seem to act as food and drink to me. This Geraldine had all these in their fullest perfection, like some strange tropical fruit that no one could imagine till they had seen. At no point was she imperfect; she was an utter little dunce, but that was her last and crowning fascination: she could not spell A B ab, and the problem of what twice thirteen was would have filled her small brown head with distraction. She could not tell you where Asia was, nor whether Japan was the capital of China; but neither could one of those delightful things we read of in the old stories, things that come out of a fountain and turn into a shower of spray when spoken to.

I was going to stay, then. What on earth made me dream of leaving *Geraldine?* Did that idea really occur to me? To leave here and get into a *railway train* and go back to a place called London—to turn back out of the seventeenth century into the horrible nineteenth century, with its railroads and smoke, and telegraphs, just because a hideous old woman called Reason had told me to do so or it would be wrong.

I took another sheet of paper and wrote.

DEAR JAMES,—I know now the reason why you sent me here. I have fallen in love with your mysterious Gerald. Leave us together and have no fear, lovers never hurt each other, except, perhaps, with kisses. I shall write to you every other day.—

Yours affectionately,

BEATRICE SINCLAIR.

This letter I gummed up in an envelope.

I had no trouble to find a stamp for it; my purse lay on the table and in it the other stamp. Then I put the letter on the mantel, and went to bed.

CHAPTER XVI

THE BLACK HORSE AND THE WHITE

I HAD such a strange dream. I dreamt that I was in man's clothes, and that I was astride of a coal black horse : how I knew that the horse was black I scarcely can tell, for the night around me was dark as death, Geraldine was on the pommel before me, grasping me round the loins with her arms ; her head was on my breast, the horse was galloping mad, mad he seemed ; behind me galloped a man on a white horse, a man in the dress of a cavalier. I turned my head now and then to look at him. He was myself, and he was dead. He swayed and he reeled in the saddle. His spurs were plunged and stuck in the white horse's sides, and great flakes of

horses bear us and bore us them through the
darkness like red flowers: we tore through
archways that seemed to rise as it is down
white roads, and through tiny hamlets with
lights that winked as it is and then we were
in the darkness again, as a mist. A
ghastly moon rose through the clouds
overhead. I looked back, he was still following, swaying and reeling, now falling far
back on the back of his horse, so that his
long black hair mixed with the horse's tail,
now falling straight forward, his hair all
thrown and mixing with the horse's mane.
I saw the nostrils of the white horse
blown out thin as paper, its staring swim-
ing eyes. Then the darkness fell again and I
named Geraldine again: and the moon broke
through again, and I saw that the white horse
had overtaken me and passed me and was
in front, and the cavalier, reeling and
swaying in the saddle held Geraldine in his
arms and they were safe dead. Then my
horse stumbled and stumbled and fell. And
I woke. All around me was in black darkness. I felt the pillows to make sure I was

bedroom, that I knew. I blew out the candle and raised the curtain. A door half open ; I pushed it and entered. On a bed, white as snow, lay a little figure curled up under the sheets. The window-blinds had not been drawn and the grey, still light fell on a small face. Never seemed anything so fast asleep as this form. As I stood watching it, it seemed to me that I could still hear the galloping of the dream horses, I felt like a thief. Geraldine was safe then ; she knew nothing of that furious ride through the night, heard none of the galloping of those horses.

As I turned from taking a last look at the sleeping face I felt awed, not exactly awed, but frightened. Do you know that perfect and absolute purity frightens one to look at, as if it were a ghost? You may laugh, but it does, though it is more rarely seen than any ghost. I have only seen it once, and that was when I saw this child asleep with the dawn on her face.

When I had found my room again I

drew up the window-blind and opened the window. The trees in the garden stood all dripping with dew in the grey light that came from the slate-coloured sky, and the chrysanthemums looked like the ghosts of chrysanthemums. Not a breath of wind. I looked up at the sky. Two crows were flying lazily in the distance, their black wings winking dreamily as they flew. Not a sound.

CHAPTER XVII

THE OLD OAK CHEST

I WOKE at nine o'clock. Someone had knocked at my door. It was only the maid-servant with hot water.

I had gone to sleep at six o'clock with the vision of that strange grey dawn in my head, and now at nine—I can never account for my motives, I seem built up of per-versities—at nine o'clock I woke, and my first sensation was one of irritation. I was irritated with myself, and I was irritated with the thoughts of the old butler. I was irritated with the window-blind which I had drawn down all crooked. I was in a sulk with Geraldine.

I looked at my face in the looking-glass. I was a fright. My eyes were red. I dressed, and I actually did not care what dress I put on.   It did not matter; all my dresses were hideous, every woman's dress was hideous, except Geraldine's, she alone knew how to dress.

Really never before had I been in such a vile and senseless humour. It seemed to take in the whole world. I passed in review all the men I had ever known. They were all about equally detestable; they seemed all so like one another, more or less hair on their faces, that was all, and yet women fall in love with these creatures; but then, what were women? I passed in review all the women I had ever known, and all the women I had ever heard of— they all had to stand for inspection beside the strange figure of Geraldine. Oh, what fools they looked, what dummies, what empty-headed apes, tricked out in borrowed feathers, full of spiteful tricks, and tricks to draw the attention of those other apes, the ones with beards.

I thought of the school-girls at the boarding-school,—those virgins so full of suppressed vice, their finnikin manners, their whispers, and their sniggers. I never thought that I too had been one of those vicious virgins.

I pricked myself with a pin, and that brought me back from my thoughts. Then I went down to breakfast. One place as usual. Old James the butler seemed grown ten years younger since that night so long ago when he let me in first, that night so long ago, the night before last. He darted about so quick that he upset a plate of muffins on the floor. Then bang! my bad humour changed suddenly to good.

What did this little wretch mean by breakfasting alone at unearthly hours? Did she have strange people out of the garden to breakfast with her? people with feet like roots, and faces like flowers. I had seen this Geraldine looking at the chrysanthemums with an expression of face as if she knew more about them than a mortal ought to know. Last night a great moth flew in from the garden, and rested quite familiarly on her hair, just above her ear. She treated the snails just as if they were kinsfolk. I felt sure that to her breakfast-table guests came who would have flown, or run, or crawled, from *my* presence.

Then, like a sombre note of music, came the recollection of my dream. I heard the mad galloping of the horses, and my good humour turned to sadness. You must think me a very changeable person, but that is just what I am. I am jotting down all my feelings as they came, so you can see that it takes very little to move me from sorrow to laughter.

I have written seventy - three pages! almost a little book. To think that I should ever have written a book, no matter how small!

Well, when breakfast was over I sat for awhile making up my mind that Geraldine might come to me before I came to her; then I got up and did exactly what I had determined not to do. I came down the toy-house corridor. I knocked at the right hand door; no answer. I pushed the door open and peeped in; no one. I knocked at the bedroom door; no answer, but I did

I

not go in, I felt somehow afraid. Then I turned to the left hand door. I opened it. It was a strangely pretty room, but it did not contain Geraldine. It looked like an oratory; the roof was arched, and at the far end the daylight through a stained glass window shone glimmering down on the polished oak floor. A silver lamp swung from the ceiling, and an oak table, plain and rather severe looking, stood in the centre. This was where she probably dined, if she ever dined, and breakfasted all alone.

What a life this strange being must have led, just like a nun, and many a morning she must have sat here all alone whilst *I* was—where ?

Do you know that all the sermons ever preached would have had less effect upon me than the sight of this room ? I suddenly saw the beastliness of the world we all live in, just as plainly as if it had been some vile reptile crawling from under that oak table ; but we never see sights like that for long, just half a second or so, and then we forget. I looked for a moment, then I turned away. Where had she gone to? was she hiding? could she be in the garden?

No, she was not in the garden; the chrysanthemums all looked as if they knew but would not tell. Oh, those chrysanthemums, how they haunt my dreams, actually haunt me; they are all dead and forgotten, but their faces seem to haunt me. Geraldine made them human when she walked amongst them, she touched their faces as if they were faces of brothers and sisters. I saw her smile at one once, and once I saw her actually frown at one of them, and now they come and haunt me as if to say, "What have you done to Geraldine?"

Then I began to feel uneasy. Where could this strange child be? had any accident befallen her? I remembered my dream, and hurried back to the house. Old James, the butler, was crossing the hall, a tray of glasses in his hands. I asked him had he seen the child, did he know where she was hiding?

He answered that she had gone out for a drive; she went at eight.

I could have boxed the old fellow's ears.

Was she in the habit of going out for drives so early in the day?

Oh, yes, several times a week the horses were ordered early. That exasperated me. So it was a habit not to be broken through on my account. Just because it was her habit, she had gone out and left me all alone, knowing very well that I would be hunting for her. Then I remembered the absurd fright I had been in about my dream, and I remembered the strange and passionate parting of the night before, and now this cold creature had gone out for a drive; no wonder she was so fond of snails.

Where was the use of loving a creature like this? it would build a house for itself of your dreams and sighs and groans, and then crawl off with its house on its back. All my waking irritation returned. I told the old butler to bring me my luncheon to my room when luncheon time came, for I felt ill—so I did—and would not come down again that day.

Then I went upstairs to my bedroom utterly determined to give Geraldine a lesson that she would never forget. She might wait for me, but I would not come, not I.

Up in my bedroom I fell into one of those stupid fits in which we—at least I do —take a tremendous amount of interest in nothing. I looked at my rings and at my hair brushes. I looked at myself in the glass. I stood with my head against the pane, look-ing out at the garden. The weather had not altered, still moist and warm and autumny ; all these three days seemed carven out of the same kind of weather so that they might last for ever as one piece, all the same, beautiful, sorrowful, and dark. " For ever " I say, for I am sure I shall see them even when I am dead : perhaps they will be for me the only solatium through eternity, given me to look at, like some gloomy but beauti-ful jewel to a sick and sorry child.

After a while I grew tired of taking an interest in nothing. I fell to wondering what Geraldine would do or say if I killed myself or was killed. She would go out for a drive very likely. Then I thought what a fool I had been to prison myself up in my bedroom and give out to the old butler that I was ill. I smoked a cigarette as I thought, and then I determined on an expedition : I would go for a prowl.

At the end of the corridor on which my bedroom opened there was a door. Yesterday morning I had opened this door to see what was behind, and had seen a staircase, a spiral staircase, that had somehow an elfish look. I told you before, I think, that on my first arrival at this house everything except the dining-room seemed familiar. Well, that feeling had utterly vanished, yet *still* everything remained familiar. I don't exactly know how to explain my meaning fully, unless I can make you understand that the ghostly part of the familiar feeling was gone.

Well, the little staircase cropped up in my mind just as I finished my cigarette, and I determined on exploring it. I looked out of my room to see that no one was about, then I came along the corridor, softly. I opened the door, and there was the little spiral staircase all covered with dust. I shut the door behind me, and I can tell you it required some courage to shut that door and remain alone in the dark with that ugly little staircase. Then up the staircase I went, feeling my way by the cold little bannister rail, till suddenly my head came bump against something. I put my hand up and felt a trap door. I pushed it, and it fell back. What a strange room I entered, perfectly square, and lit by one dusty window. The walls were hung with arras, and the only piece of furniture was a large black oak chest, carved all over with foliage and figures. It stood opposite the window.

Somehow this room had a strangely forlorn and melancholy appearance, it had also a vague and musty smell. The arras looked ghostly. Perhaps it was the perfect silence, but it appeared to me that here a horse and there a stag seemed ready to jump from the canvas.

I sat down on the oak chest, and began to observe the tapestry more attentively. Beginning at the window, my eye ran along it. Here was a hunting scene—a meet evidently—ever so many horsemen surrounding a man on a white horse, he seemed the chief; he was dressed as a cavalier, his hair was black and flowing. Beyond, in the distance, lay a castle, a castle on a green hill, with a white pathway running down it. I knew that castle was meant to represent Castle Sinclair. A little further on another scene. The same cavalier, riding, and by his side a lady on a brown horse; how proudly the horses stepped. A little further on another scene, love this time, and the same man and the same woman; they were kissing.

Then I knew by a kind of intuition that this tapestry was meant to represent the connection of the houses of Wilder and

Sinclair, worked, probably, through long generations by the pious hands of Wilder women.

Suddenly I got up and looked at the tapestry just behind me. Yes, the same man and the same woman—she on a couch, he on the floor, perhaps dead, a broken glass beside him. Was that the poison running on the tapestry-wrought floor?— perhaps. The next scene was a funeral procession; black nodding plumes and bowed heads.

I looked no more; that tapestry gave me the shivers.

I turned to the oak chest and raised the lid; an odour of rosemary filled the air. I peeped in. Down at the bottom lay some clothes, carefully folded, on the clothes a sword, and on the sword a great cavalier's hat with a magnificent black feather; I took out the hat and sword, and laid them on the floor, then I took out a most exquisite amber satin doublet, and the other parts of a man's dress. Down at the bottom still there lay a pair of long buff-coloured boots, with silver spurs, and a great glittering silver trumpet, to which was attached a long crimson silk cord.

I would have clapped my hands, only my arms were so full; here was everything I wanted. That little Puritan with the pale face would whimper no more for jingling spurs and a sword on her lover. Oh! the good sword! I drew it from its sheath, and looked at its broad, strong blade, all damascened near the hilt, then I popped it back in its sheath, and kicked off my shoe. I wanted to see if the boots would fit; I tried one on, it fitted to perfection. This cavalier, whoever he was, must have had an amazingly small foot. Perhaps he was Gerald Wilder. Nothing more likely, for this room seemed dedicated to him, and these things were possibly his relics; any way, they were mine for the present, and I promised myself a fine masquerade.

What would Geraldine say when she saw me?

I took out the trumpet; it looked like a

battle-trumpet ; there was a dint upon it
as if from a blow. It was solid silver, and
was marked near the mouthpiece with a
little tiger and a P surmounted by a tiny star.
It was evidently intended to be slung
round the back by the silken cord, so I
slung it round my back, and taking all the
other things, I left the room, laden like an
old clothes man. I had fearful work shut-
ting the trap door with all the things in my
arms, but I managed it at last, and got
safely back to my bedroom without having
been seen.

On the dressing-table stood a silver tray
with some luncheon and a decanter of
sherry ; so the old butler had been. I
shut the door and locked it, then I placed
all my booty on the bed, and sat down
to eat what the old fellow had brought
me.

As I ate I thought how fortunate it was
that there were so few servants. The only
ones I had seen indoors were the butler and
the sour-faced maid. There must have been
a cook, and a very good one, hidden down

stairs somewhere, but she, or he, was never visible. How, thought I, do these two manage to keep this great house in order? they are always working like galley slaves, I suppose, and Wilder pays them like princes; anyhow I am very glad, two are quite enough, almost two too many.

Then I rose and placed the luncheon things on the floor out of my way, and then I took all the hairpins out of my hair and let it fall as it always wants to fall, right round my shoulders in black, curling locks. Then I undressed. I laughed as I put on the man's things, but my heart was fluttering fearfully lest they shouldn't fit. I shall never forget the perfume of rosemary from the amber satin doublet as I drew it on. Then the boots, how the spurs jingled; but I would not look at myself in the glass yet, I was not perfect, for the sword still lay on the bed, and the trumpet. I buckled the sword-belt and swung the trumpet behind me, then with one hand on the hilt of my sword and one hand on my hip I whirled round on my heel to face my image in the cheval glass. I can never tell you, nor could you ever imagine, the deep, the *furious* pride that filled me as I gazed at the glorious-looking man who faced me in the mirror. Can you imagine an eagle condemned into being a sparrow; can you imagine the feelings of that eagle should it find itself once more an eagle royal and splendid? So great, so overmastering was this feeling, that I utterly forgot Geraldine and the whole world that held her.

I was myself again, yet I was completely changed. All my waywardness and woman's pettinesses seemed vanished and drowned. As I looked at the cavalier with black flowing hair, I smiled, and he smiled. How gloomy and stern was that smile. What a graceful, and strange, and poetic-looking man he was; one could imagine him riding through a battle with his face unmoved, one could imagine him terrible in love.

And he was *I*.

Then I turned and threw myself into an

arm-chair. Geraldine had just entered my mind, and the stern cavalier, who would have laughed in the face of a battle, became like a child. Do men turn weak like this before the image of their love? I veritably believe they do.

"Geraldine," I thought, "she went out; ah, yes, this morning. I shall go to her when it is dusk. Will she smile, or will she frown, and my white rose will she wear it? Then I found myself wondering what rose. I could not remember actually that I had given her a rose, yet a vague impression filled my mind that I had. Somewhere long ago I had given her a rose, and my fate seemed to depend on whether she would wear this rose, now, this evening.

Oh, I tell you, on that afternoon, ay, and ever since I put on the dress of the cavalier, I was not and am not—what I was. That dress seemed to seal a compact, and I was, and am still, partly drunk with the remembrance of a dim and shadowy past.

I sat in the arm-chair thinking; time must have flown as it never flew before.

I would go to her with the dusk and behold it was dusk!

And the wind had risen with the dusk and was sighing amidst the garden trees like a ghost.

CHAPTER XVIII

THE TRUMPETER

I ROSE from the arm-chair, and I stood, I remember, sucking in my underlip and staring at the floor. Then I turned to the wardrobe, and took out my great sealskin cloak. I threw it round me and it reached to my feet. I wished to conceal my clothes, why, I did not exactly know, but it seemed to me that they ought to be hidden from everyone but Geraldine.

Then I opened the bedroom door softly and peeped into the passage. No one— not a sound. I stole down the corridor to the head of the great staircase, and peeped over into the hall, the lamps were not yet lit. Then I came down the staircase so softly that you might have thought me a shadow only for the faint, silvery jingle of the spurs. I entered the corridor, and the heavy silk curtain fell behind me. Then I found myself standing at the right hand door with my hand pressed to my heart. No actor about to enter before his audience could have felt the nervousness I felt. My heart seemed gone mad. Then I dropped my sealskin cloak and my nervousness fell with it. I tossed my hair back, felt the hilt of my sword, and without knocking, I turned the door handle and entered.

The figure of a girl stood at the open window; she was gazing out at the dusk-stricken garden. Then she turned and saw me. I heard her breath caught back, and I saw in her hand a white rose.

Did I cross the room? I must have crossed it, but I have no recollection of doing so. I knew nothing of the world or the things in the world, save a face that was trying to hide itself on my shoulder, and a voice that was whispering "You have come." Yes, one other thing I knew. A beetle passed by out some-

K

where in the garden, and the dreamy and mournful boom of his wings mixed sadly with my intoxication, seeming like a voice from long ages ago.

Oh, that meeting in the grey autumn dusk, that voice repeating over and over again the words "You have come." When shall I hear those words again? Never, There is no perhaps for me, I know in some strange way that I shall hear those words again—never. And the fault is mine.

CHAPTER XIX

THE TRUMPETER

THE fault is mine, for I knew, and Geraldine knew nothing.

I knew the past. I knew of my sin. I knew, by some instinct, that God had brought the past to me. As a means of redeeming my crime He had imposed re-nunciation upon me as a penance, and I had chosen instead of renunciation this deathly masquerade. I would not be debased, I would not be humbled. God help me—I am humble enough now. All that is what I see now ; just then I saw nothing and cared for nothing but Geraldine.

We kissed only once, just like two frightened children, then we both passed into the garden. Geraldine's arm I had drawn round my waist. We wandered, locked together, through the dusk of the garden. We found the dark yew tree walk by instinct ; there was a seat and we sat down. We could scarcely see each other, we were utterly dumb, confounded with love.

We heard the wind pass by : we heard the dew fall, and the crying of the night-bird—a hooting sound.

The rest of that evening I only remember in silhouettes, just as a drunkard remembers his drunkenness. I remember the parting. I remember it well, for I saw it reflected in a long mirror. Across the room where we had been sitting, I can see the picture still—a cavalier standing by a girl.

Then I found myself in my bedroom all alone, the clock on the mantel striking twelve. The window-sash was open : the clouds had all broken up, and the moon was shining on the trees. I leaned on the sill, my head supported on my right hand, my left hand on the hilt of my sword. I listened. The wind was sighing amongst the trees, and on the wind I heard

something far away and strange. A con-
fused noise, it seemed like the noise of
a battle in the distance. I tossed back my
hair, and my left hand worked at the hilt
of my sword. Yes, it must be a battle,
a great battle in the distance. I caught
the cry, "Sinclair, Sinclair," and then a
cry like the distant sound of a thousand
voices, "For the King." I heard the far-
off tramp of horses, the vague cries, the
clash of steel. Then the imperious call
of a trumpet, the call of a battle-trumpet.
I sprung to my feet from my stooping
attitude. I swung the trumpet from behind
me, and seizing it, placed the silver mouthpiece to my lips; then I blew. I blew
till the rafters rang and the ceiling shook.
I paused, then again I blew. I was
drunk, and mad, mad—with the madness of
battle. I left the room. The soul of the
trumpet seemed to have possessed me, the
mad sound of the trumpet beaten back from
the walls drove me onwards. Through the
corridor, down the great staircase, across
the hall, then back up the staircase, along

the corridor to my room I passed, the whole house ringing to the sound of the silver trumpet.

Then I found myself lying on my bed-room floor, sick, faint, and covered with a cold perspiration. The trumpet lay beside me. Away upstairs I thought I heard frightened cries, and the banging of a door, then silence. I crawled to the bed. I could scarcely drag my body on to it, my exhaustion was so great. Then I fell into a deep and dreamless sleep.

CHAPTER XX

THE RUBY WINE

OH, the dismal dawn that woke me, it came through the window that I had left wide open. I sat up in bed. I was still dressed. My spurs had torn the coverlet, the trumpet and its blood-red silken cord lay upon the floor. The wind blew in, shaking the curtains mournfully. I saw it all at a glance. I remembered everything—the trumpeter had returned. Oh, it was awful, that moment of cringing terror. It seemed as if fate had been crawling at me slowly during the last three days. It seemed as if last night she had made a fearful bound, and now, like a tiger, was crouching for the final spring.

I had done it with my own lips, I had blown the death-trumpet for Geraldine. And now that voice came back that I heard at first, saying, "Remember, Geraldine is a boy." Ah, yes, I remembered it now, now that I had heralded to Geraldine the fate to which all the eldest boys of the Wilder family were doomed.

I threw myself face down on the pillows, weeping as if my heart would break ; but of what use were tears ? I had elected to play the part of a man, tears were out of place. I stopped weeping and dried my eyes. *What* was to be done ? how could I save this child ?

" Only one way," said a voice in my head, " leave her—you alone can kill her, so leave her."

I would,—I would leave her. I determined on that and rose from the bed ; but, oh God help me, I determined to go first to her to say good-bye. Was it wrong ? ask it of yourself. How—how could I leave this child, whose life was dearer to me than my own, how could I leave her without saying good-bye ? Do you know what it means to leave a person you love, to leave for ever without saying good-bye ? Could a mother leave her infant never

to see it again without first kissing its tiny
hands, its lips, its eyes? I could have torn
my heart out with my own hands, but I
could not have left Geraldine without saying
good-bye.

I came to the great pier-glass and I saw
myself—the cavalier. I leaned my head
against it and against his, and I gazed out
of the window at the dull grey sky; still
another day of the damp, dark, sorrowful
weather. The clock on the mantel pointed
to the hour—quarter to six.

" I shall kiss her once and say good-bye
and leave her for ever," I murmured to
myself, but the words seemed to have little
meaning. " I shall go to her now," I said,
standing upright and addressing my own
reflection in the glass, " for the sooner it is
over the better."

I left the room. The passage was dark,
but I felt my way with my hand. Down the
stairs I came, across the hall, down the
little corridor. I lifted the curtain and
knocked. " Come in," said a voice.

She was not asleep, then. I opened the

door. Geraldine was sitting by the open window, dressed ; she had not been to bed. The bed lay white—Oh, God, if these tears would only choke me and not fill my throat with this dull, heavy pain—white and uncrumpled. She stretched out her arms to me feebly and as if against her will. And now I had kissed her three times, and was kneeling by her side, I—who had determined to kiss her once and leave her— and her head was upon my shoulder, and she was telling me how she could not go to bed for thinking of me, and how she loved me, loved me as no one had ever been loved before. Oh the innocence and divine sweetness of this love, of this voice, and the terror and anguish of the thought, " You are doomed to kill her, doomed, doomed."

How could I leave her ? She had actually put her arm round my neck. I laid my head behind hers, so that I might not see the dawn, and might forget the world. My lips kept murmuring, " It is fate." As if in answer to the muttering of my lips there

came a sound, the turret clock was striking
six, six melancholy strokes; they brought
back to my mind the words of the little
black book.

"Geraldine," I cried, holding my face on
her knees, "it was this hour, long, long ago,
when I killed you; tell me to go, tell me to
leave you, it will happen again, for Death
is here, oh! *listen* to the wind." I ceased,
and the wind sobbed and sighed in the
garden, but no word came from Geraldine,
only a tear that fell and burned my hand.
"Geraldine," I whispered, "I have betrayed
you, turn me away for your own sake."

Then I felt two soft hands seize my hair
on either side of my head, and lift my face.
I heard a voice whisper, "You are mine, and
I will hold you so."

"Ah! then," I cried, "let the past be gone
for ever; now, now with this kiss—and this—
and this—let us defy Death." But even as
our lips clung together, the wind moaned
drearily in the trees. I heard Death, I felt
him, he was in the garden, his gray misty
face was at the window. We clung to each

other like people drowning ; we seemed to know that the eternal parting was so near ; speechless, with lips paralysed, but still pressed together, we seemed listening for help, but no help came, nor sound—only the sound of the wind mourning in the trees.

Then drearily a little bird began to sing somewhere in the garden. Its song pierced my wretched heart and drove me to madness, to passion. I stood up, and, as my arms were round her, I lifted her in my arms. For one moment I held that delightful burthen, so warm and supple and perfumed, then growing dizzy, I laid her on the bed and leaned beside her. She started and drew back from something she saw in my gaze. Her lips grew pale.

"Geraldine," I muttered, "what is the matter, *Geraldine ?*"

The pale lips moved, and a terror shot through me. She was going to faint ; no, she was not going to faint, she seemed recovered now, but how weak she seemed.

"Wait," I whispered to her, "wait till I come back."

I left the room and hurried across the hall to the dining-room. Here, on the sideboard was a lock-up case containing brandy and liqueurs, but it was locked, of course ; here was a decanter labelled " Roussillon." That would do.

I took a wine-glass and the decanter, and returned.

Geraldine, when she saw the decanter, shook her head, just as children shake their heads at the medicine bottle. But I was firm, and poured out a glass of the ruby wine. I put my hand behind her head and told her she must drink, drink it right off. She did as she was bid, and made a face ; she said it was, bitter, and I said " Nonsense." Then her eyes became sleepy, and she lay with them fixed on mine ; then her eyelids began to droop with sleep. Oh, how jealous I felt of sleep. And now I could not see her eyes at all. She was breathing deeply, and her lips now and then gave a little twitch. I sat holding her hand and stroking it. I sat for twenty minutes watching her. How light her breathing had suddenly become, and now suddenly she caught her breath and smiled as if she beheld some one in her dreams. I heard the galloping of a horse from the avenue, but I did not heed.

I waited for the next breath, but it never came. The smile had parted her lips, but she did not breathe; the eyelids lifted a tiny bit, but the eyes did not seem to see.

I said " Geraldine." No answer.

What was that furious ringing of bells, and that thundering as at a door ? I heard it, but never heeded.

" Geraldine, Geraldine," I whispered. " Geraldine, wake, I am waiting for you." No answer, but the sound of the wind wailing in the trees.

She never moved, the smile on her face never changed. I sobbed. I turned round. Wilder was entering the room, he had just arrived. When he saw me dressed as I was he threw up his hands. He did not look at the form on the bed; he looked at

the decanter, he smelt the glass, and he
gave a little senile, dreary kind of laugh.
He pointed to it and made a motion as
if drinking. I knew what he meant,—it
was one of his opium decanters mislabled
Roussillon.

Then he sat down by the form on the
bed, with his hands on his knees and his
head bowed, and I heard him murmuring
the words " My child."

The turret clock struck seven ; with the
last stroke I heard the shrill neigh of a
horse, and the sound of a hoof striking
sharply on granite.

It was as if to say : the play is ended,
the curtain has fallen, never, never to rise
again.

CHAPTER XXI

"AND THEY LAID HIM TO HIS REST"

I REMEMBER next being in my own bed-room. I was taking off the cavalier's dress, and I felt like a traveller who had returned from some far and beautiful land. I never wept, nor even sighed. And I remember the rest of that strange and ghostly day, the silence of the house, and the room beyond the pretty corridor that held a thing stranger than anything on earth or in the sea. It rained slightly towards dusk. I was looking out of a window on to the garden, later—it may have been midnight for aught I know, I came down the painted corridor, and entered the bedroom. A lamp was burning, and on the bed lay something small and straight, covered with a sheet. I drew away the sheet, and saw the face I had known

160

so well; just the same it looked, only smaller and more helpless, and the smile had faded away into a vague, beseeching look.

Then I remember days that passed, and one day when Wilder said to me, "You will not come?" "Where?" I asked. "To the graveyard."

I was in the library when he spoke. I shook my head.

He left the room; and a little later I heard heavy footsteps, and the tolling of a bell in the distance. I counted, one, two, three—sixteen, then the bell ceased.

CHAPTER XXII

THE END

" —And the ballade humbly prays,
 The tribute of your sighs,
For the hawke's blinde little eyes,
 —And the cavalier who lies
By the four cross ways."

THE little falcon came back last night. It
has been weeks away, but it came back last
night, and I feel it even now pinching at
my wrist. It seems to say, " Hurry, you
have nearly finished." It seems anxious for
me to go with it. Where? I do not know.

I can scarcely write. I am half-blind
with what? God only knows. Not tears, for
I have no tears left. A darkness has stolen
over my brain. In writing this story I
have drawn the past up to me like an un-
willing ghost : I have kissed it on the forehead, mouth, and eyes, and now that my

story is finished it has slipped back into the darkness, and I am left alone.

They have buried Geraldine. Not in the little church in the park, where all the Wilders are buried; she has a grave of her own outside the church, and on the marble headstone is the name " Beatrice Sinclair."

But I shall be buried in the church, and I know that my tablet will bear the inscription, " Sir Gerald Wilder, Kt.," so that even our dust may not meet,—what matter ?

I am not afraid to die ; in fact, if I could be glad about anything, I should now be glad. Death seems to me such a little withered, contemptible figure, for ever jealous of Love—yet sometimes death seems to me like a white marble portico, seen down an alley of cypress trees, under a sky all dark with autumn.

Beneath the ocean spray
Strange things lie hid away ;
And in the gloom
Of many a tomb
Lie stranger things than they.
But in the world, I wis,
Nought is more strange than this—
The love of Death for May.
Nothing more strange above
The skies where eagles rove ;
Nothing below the winter snow
Or flowers that spring winds move ;
Nought in eternity
Or time, unless it be
The love of Death for Love.

TURNBULL AND SPEARS, PRINTERS, EDINBURGH.

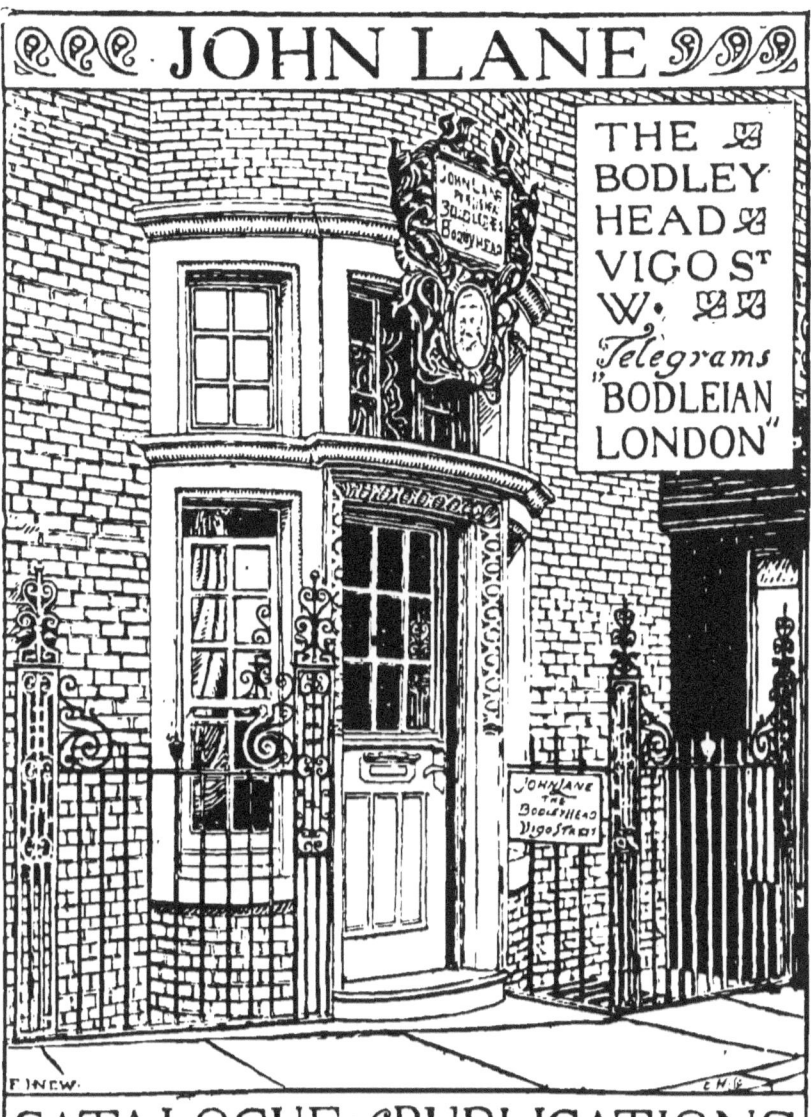

JOHN LANE

THE BODLEY HEAD VIGO St W.

Telegrams "BODLEIAN LONDON"

CATALOGUE of PUBLICATIONS in BELLES LETTRES all at net prices

List of Books

IN

BELLES LETTRES

Published by John Lane

The Bodley Head

VIGO STREET, LONDON, W.

Adams (Francis).
ESSAYS IN MODERNITY. Crown 8vo.
5s. net. [*Shortly.*]
A CHILD OF THE AGE. (*See* KEY-
NOTES SERIES.)

A. E.
HOMEWARD SONGS BY THE WAY.
Sq. 16mo, wrappers. 1s. 6d. net.
Transferred to the present Pub-
lisher. [*Second Edition.*]
THE EARTH BREATH, AND OTHER
POEMS. [*In preparation.*]

Aldrich (T. B.)
LATER LYRICS. Sm. Fcap. 8vo.
2s. 6d. net.

Allen (Grant).
THE LOWER SLOPES: A Volume of
Verse. With Title-page and Cover
Design by J. ILLINGWORTH KAY.
Crown 8vo. 5s. net.
THE WOMAN WHO DID. (*See* KEY-
NOTES SERIES.)
THE BRITISH BARBARIANS. (*See*
KEYNOTES SERIES.)

Arcady Library (The).
A Series of Open-Air Books. Edited
by J. S. FLETCHER. With Cover
Designs by PATTEN WILSON.
Each volume crown 8vo. 5s. net.
I. ROUND ABOUT A BRIGHTON
COACH OFFICE. By MAUDE
EGERTON KING. With
over 30 Illustrations by
LUCY KEMP-WELCH.
II. LIFE IN ARCADIA. By J. S.
FLETCHER. With 20 Illus-
trations by PATTEN WIL-
SON

Arcady Library (The)—*cont.*
III. SCHOLAR GIPSIES. By JOHN
BUCHAN. With 7 full-page
Etchings by D.Y. CAMERON
IV. IN THE GARDEN OF PEACE.
By HELEN MILMAN. With
24 Illustrations by EDMUND
H. NEW.
V. THE HAPPY EXILE. By H.
D. LOWRY. With 6 Etch-
ings by E. PHILIP PIMLOTT.
[*In preparation.*]

Beeching (Rev. H. C.).
IN A GARDEN: Poems. With Title-
page designed by ROGER FRY.
Crown 8vo. 5s. net.
ST. AUGUSTINE AT OSTIA. Crown
8vo, wrappers. 1s. net.

Beerbohm (Max).
THE WORKS OF MAX BEERBOHM.
With a Bibliography by JOHN
LANE. Sq. 16mo. 4s. 6d. net.

Benson (Arthur Christopher)
LYRICS. Fcap. 8vo, buckram. 5s.
net.
LORD VYET AND OTHER POEMS.
Fcap. 8vo. 3s. 6d. net.

**Bodley Head Anthologies
(The).**
Edited by ROBERT H. CASE. With
Title-page and Cover Designs by
WALTER WEST. Each volume
crown 8vo. 5s. net.
I. ENGLISH EPITHALAMIES.
By ROBERT H. CASE.

Bodley Head Anthologies (The)—*continued.*

II. MUSA PISCATRIX. By JOHN BUCHAN. With 6 Etchings by E. PHILIP PIMLOTT.

III. ENGLISH ELEGIES. By JOHN C. BAILEY.
[*In preparation.*

IV. ENGLISH SATIRES. By CHAS. HILL DICK.
[*In preparation.*

Bridges (Robert).
SUPPRESSED CHAPTERS AND OTHER BOOKISHNESS. Crown 8vo. 3s. 6d. net. [*Second Edition.*

Brotherton (Mary).
ROSEMARY FOR REMEMBRANCE. With Title-page and Cover Design by WALTER WEST. Fcap. 8vo. 3s. 6d. net.

Crackanthorpe (Hubert).
VIGNETTES. A Miniature Journal of Whim and Sentiment. Fcap. 8vo, boards. 2s. 6d. net.

Crane (Walter).
TOY BOOKS. Re-issue, each with new Cover Design and End Papers. This LITTLE PIG'S PICTURE BOOK, containing:
I. THIS LITTLE PIG.
II. THE FAIRY SHIP.
III. KING LUCKIEBOY'S PARTY.

The three bound in one volume with a decorative cloth cover, end papers, and a newly written and designed preface and title-page. 3s. 6d. net; separately 9d. net each.

MOTHER HUBBARD'S PICTURE BOOK, containing:
I. MOTHER HUBBARD'S.
II. THE THREE BEARS.
III. THE ABSURD A. B. C.

The three bound in one volume with a decorative cloth cover, end papers, and a newly written and designed preface and title-page. 3s. 6d. net; separately 9d. net each.

Custance (Olive).
OPALS: Poems. Fcap. 8vo. 3s. 6d. net.

Dalmon (C. W.).
SONG FAVOURS. With a Title-page by J. P. DONNE. Sq. 16mo. 3s. 6d. net.

Davidson (John).
PLAYS: An Unhistorical Pastoral; A Romantic Farce; Bruce, a Chronicle Play; Smith, a Tragic Farce; Scaramouch in Naxos, a Pantomime. With a Frontispiece and Cover Design by AUBREY BEARDSLEY. Small 4to. 7s. 6d. net.

FLEET STREET ECLOGUES. Fcap. 8vo, buckram. 4s. 6d. net.
[*Third Edition.*

FLEET STREET ECLOGUES. 2nd Series. Fcap. 8vo, buckram. 4s. 6d. net. [*Second Edition.*

A RANDOM ITINERARY AND A BALLAD. With a Frontispiece and Title-page by LAURENCE HOUSMAN. Fcap. 8vo, Irish Linen. 5s. net.

BALLADS AND SONGS. With a Title-page and Cover Design by WALTER WEST. Fcap. 8vo, buckram. 5s. net. [*Fourth Edition.*

NEW BALLADS. Fcap. 8vo, buckram. 4s. 6d. net. [*Second Edition.*

De Tabley (Lord).
POEMS, DRAMATIC AND LYRICAL. By JOHN LEICESTER WARREN (Lord de Tabley). Illustrations and Cover Design by C. S. RICKETTS. Crown 8vo. 7s. 6d. net. [*Third Edition.*

POEMS, DRAMATIC AND LYRICAL. Second Series, uniform in binding with the former volume. Crown 8vo. 5s. net.

Duer (Caroline, and Alice).
POEMS. Fcap. 8vo. 3s. 6d. net.

Egerton (George)
KEYNOTES. (*See* KEYNOTES SERIES.)

DISCORDS. (*See* KEYNOTES SERIES.)

YOUNG OFEG'S DITTIES. A translation from the Swedish of OLA HANSSON. With Title-page and Cover Design by AUBREY BEARDSLEY. Crown 8vo. 3s. 6d. net.

SYMPHONIES. [*In preparation.*

Eglinton (John).

TWO ESSAYS ON THE REMNANT. Post 8vo, wrappers. 1s. 6d net. *Transferred to the present Publisher.* [*Second Edition.*

Eve's Library.

Each volume, crown 8vo. 3s. 6d. net.

I. MODERN WOMEN. An English rendering of LAURA MARHOLM HANSSON'S "DAS BUCH DER FRAUEN" by HERMIONE RAMSDEN. Subjects: Sonia Kovalevsky, George Egerton, Eleanora Duse, Amalie Skram, Marie Bashkirtseff, A. Ch. Edgren Lefler.

II. THE ASCENT OF WOMAN. By ROY DEVEREUX.

III. MARRIAGE QUESTIONS IN MODERN FICTION. By ELIZABETH RACHEL CHAPMAN.

Fea (Allan).

THE FLIGHT OF THE KING: a full, true, and particular account of the escape of His Most Sacred Majesty King Charles II. after the Battle of Worcester, with Sixteen Portraits in Photogravure and nearly 100 other Illustrations. Demy 8vo. 21s. net.

Field (Eugene).

THE LOVE AFFAIRS OF A BIBLIOMANIAC. Post 8vo. 3s. 6d. net.

Fletcher (J. S.).

THE WONDERFUL WAPENTAKE. By "A SON OF THE SOIL." With 18 full-page Illustrations by J. A. SYMINGTON. Crown 8vo. 5s. 6d. net.

LIFE IN ARCADIA. (*See* ARCADY LIBRARY.)

GOD'S FAILURES. (*See* KEYNOTES SERIES.)

BALLADS OF REVOLT. Sq. 32mo. 2s. 6d. net.

Ford (James L.).

THE LITERARY SHOP AND OTHER TALES. Fcap. 8vo. 3s. 6d. net.

Four-and-Sixpenny Novels.

Each volume with Title-page and Cover Design by PATTEN WILSON. Crown 8vo. 4s. 6d. net.

GALLOPING DICK. By H. B. MARRIOTT WATSON.

THE WOOD OF THE BRAMBLES. By FRANK MATHEW.

THE SACRIFICE OF FOOLS. By R. MANIFOLD CRAIG.

A LAWYER'S WIFE. By Sir NEVILL GEARY, Bart. [*Second Edition.*

WEIGHED IN THE BALANCE. By HARRY LANDER.

GLAMOUR. By META ORRED.

PATIENCE SPARHAWK AND HER TIMES. By GERTRUDE ATHERTON.

THE WISE AND THE WAYWARD. By G. S. STREET.

The following are in preparation :

MIDDLE GREYNESS. By A. J. DAWSON.

DERELICTS. By W. J. LOCKE.

THE MARTYR'S BIBLE. By GEORGE FIFTH.

A CELIBATE'S WIFE. By HERBERT FLOWERDEW.

MAX. By JULIAN CROSKEY.

THE MAKING OF A PRIG. By EVELYN SHARP.

THE TREE OF LIFE. By NETTA SYRETT.

CECILIA. By STANLEY V. MAKOWER.

Fuller (H. B.).

THE PUPPET BOOTH. Twelve Plays. Crown 8vo. 4s. 6d. net.

Gale (Norman).

ORCHARD SONGS. With Title-page and Cover Design by J. ILLINGWORTH KAY. Fcap. 8vo, Irish Linen. 5s. net.

Also a Special Edition limited in number on hand-made paper bound in English vellum. £1 1s. net.

Garnett (Richard).

POEMS. With Title-page by J. ILLINGWORTH KAY. Crown 8vo. 5s. net.

DANTE, PETRARCH, CAMOENS, cxxiv Sonnets, rendered in English. With Title-page by PATTEN WILSON. Crown 8vo. 5s. net.

Gibson (Charles Dana).

DRAWINGS: Eighty-Five Large Cartoons. Oblong Folio. 15s. net.

Gibson (Charles Dana)—
continued.

PICTURES OF PEOPLE. Eighty-Five Large Cartoons. Oblong folio. 15s. net.

Gosse (Edmund).

THE LETTERS OF THOMAS LOVELL BEDDOES. Now first edited. Pott 8vo. 5s. net.
Also 25 copies large paper. 12s. 6d. net

Grahame (Kenneth).

PAGAN PAPERS. With Title-page by AUBREY BEARDSLEY. Fcap. 8vo. 5s. net.
[*Out of Print at present.*
THE GOLDEN AGE. With Cover Design by CHARLES ROBINSON. Crown 8vo. 3s. 6d. net.
[*Fifth Edition.*

Greene (G. A.).

ITALIAN LYRISTS OF TO-DAY. Translations in the original metres from about thirty-five living Italian poets, with bibliographical and biographical notes. Crown 8vo. 5s. net.

Greenwood (Frederick).

IMAGINATION IN DREAMS. Crown 8vo. 5s. net.

Hake (T. Gordon).

A SELECTION FROM HIS POEMS. Edited by Mrs. MEYNELL. With a Portrait after D. G. ROSSETTI, and a Cover Design by GLEESON WHITE. Crown 8vo. 5s. net.

Hayes (Alfred).

THE VALE OF ARDEN AND OTHER POEMS. With a Title-page and a Cover designed by E. H. NEW. Fcap. 8vo. 3s. 6d. net.
Also 25 copies large paper. 15s. net.

Hazlitt (William).

LIBER AMORIS; OR, THE NEW PYGMALION. Edited, with an Introduction, by RICHARD LE GALLIENNE. To which is added an exact transcript of the original MS., Mrs. Hazlitt's Diary in Scotland, and letters never before published. Portrait after BEWICK, and facsimile letters. 400 Copies only. 4to, 364 pp., buckram. 21s. net.

Heinemann (William).

THE FIRST STEP; A Dramatic Moment. Small 4to. 3s. 6d. net.

Hopper (Nora).

BALLAD IN PROSE. With a Title-page and Cover by WALTER WEST. Sq. 16mo. 5s. net.
UNDER QUICKEN BOUGHS. With Title-page designed by PATTEN WILSON, and Cover designed by ELIZABETH NAYLOR. Crown 8vo. 5s. net.

Housman (Clemence).

THE WERE WOLF. With 6 full-page Illustrations, Title-page, and Cover Design by LAURENCE HOUSMAN. Sq. 16mo. 3s. 6d. net.

Housman (Laurence).

GREEN ARRAS: Poems. With 6 Illustrations, Title-page, Cover Design, and End Papers by the Author. Crown 8vo. 5s. net.
GODS AND THEIR MAKERS. Crown 8vo, 3s. 6d. net. [*In preparation.*

Irving (Laurence).

GODEFROI AND YOLANDE: A Play. Sm. 4to. 3s. 6d. net.
[*In preparation.*

James (W. P.)

ROMANTIC PROFESSIONS: A Volume of Essays. With Title-page designed by J. ILLINGWORTH KAY. Crown 8vo. 5s. net.

Johnson (Lionel).

THE ART OF THOMAS HARDY: Six Essays. With Etched Portrait by WM. STRANG, and Bibliography by JOHN LANE. Crown 8vo. 5s. 6d. net. [*Second Edition.*
Also 150 copies, large paper, with proofs of the portrait. £1 1s. net.

Johnson (Pauline).

WHITE WAMPUM: Poems. With a Title-page and Cover Design by E. H. NEW. Crown 8vo. 5s. net.

Johnstone (C. E.).

BALLADS OF BOY AND BEAK. With a Title-page by F. H. TOWNSEND. Sq. 32mo. 2s. net.

Kemble (E. W.)

KEMBLE'S COONS. 30 Drawings of Coloured Children and Southern Scenes. Large 4to. 5s. net.

Keynotes Series.

Each volume with specially-designed Title-page by AUBREY BEARDS-LEY or PATTEN WILSON. Crown 8vo, cloth. 3s. 6d. net.

I. KEYNOTES. By GEORGE EGERTON.
[*Seventh Edition.*

II. THE DANCING FAUN. By FLORENCE FARR.

III. POOR FOLK. Translated from the Russian of F. Dostoievsky by LENA MILMAN. With a Preface by GEORGE MOORE.

IV. A CHILD OF THE AGE. By FRANCIS ADAMS.

V. THE GREAT GOD PAN AND THE INMOST LIGHT. By ARTHUR MACHEN.
[*Second Edition.*

VI. DISCORDS. By GEORGE EGERTON.
[*Fifth Edition.*

VII. PRINCE ZALESKI. By M. P. SHIEL.

VIII. THE WOMAN WHO DID. By GRANT ALLEN.
[*Twenty-second Edition.*

IX. WOMEN'S TRAGEDIES. By H. D. LOWRY.

X. GREY ROSES. By HENRY HARLAND.

XI. AT THE FIRST CORNER AND OTHER STORIES. By H. B. MARRIOTT WATSON.

XII. MONOCHROMES. By ELLA D'ARCY.

XIII. AT THE RELTON ARMS. By EVELYN SHARP.

XIV. THE GIRL FROM THE FARM. By GERTRUDE DIX.
[*Second Edition.*

XV. THE MIRROR OF MUSIC. By STANLEY V. MAKOWER.

XVI. YELLOW AND WHITE. By W. CARLTON DAWE.

XVII. THE MOUNTAIN LOVERS. By FIONA MACLEOD.

XVIII. THE WOMAN WHO DIDN'T. By VICTORIA CROSSE.
[*Third Edition.*

Keynotes Series—*continued.*

XIX. THE THREE IMPOSTORS. By ARTHUR MACHEN.

XX. NOBODY'S FAULT. By NETTA SYRETT.
[*Second Edition.*

XXI. THE BRITISH BARBARIANS. By GRANT ALLEN.
[*Second Edition.*

XXII. IN HOMESPUN. By E. NESBIT.

XXIII. PLATONIC AFFECTIONS. By JOHN SMITH.

XXIV. NETS FOR THE WIND. By UNA TAYLOR.

XXV. WHERE THE ATLANTIC MEETS THE LAND. By CALDWELL LIPSETT.

XXVI. IN SCARLET AND GREY. By FLORENCE HENNIKER. (With THE SPECTRE OF THE REAL by FLORENCE HENNIKER and THOMAS HARDY.)
[*Second Edition.*

XXVII. MARIS STELLA. By MARIE CLOTHILDE BALFOUR.

XXVIII. DAY BOOKS. By MABEL E. WOTTON.

XXIX. SHAPES IN THE FIRE. By M. P. SHIEL.

XXX. UGLY IDOL. By CLAUD NICHOLSON.

XXXI. KAKEMONOS. By W. CARLTON DAWE.

XXXII. GOD'S FAILURES. By J. S. FLETCHER.

XXXIII. MERE SENTIMENT. By A. J. DAWSON.

XXXIV. A DELIVERANCE. By ALLAN MONKHOUSE.
[*In preparation.*

Lane's Library.

Each volume crown 8vo. 3s. 6d. net.

I. MARCH HARES. By HAROLD FREDERIC.
[*Second Edition.*

II. THE SENTIMENTAL SEX. By GERTRUDE WARDEN.

III. GOLD. By ANNIE LINDEN.

Lane's Library—*continued.*

The following are in preparation:

IV. BROKEN AWAY. By BEA-
TRICE GRIMSHAW.

V. A MAN FROM THE NORTH.
By E. A. BENNETT.

VI. THE DUKE OF LINDEN. By
JOSEPH F. CHARLES.

Leather (R. K.).

VERSES. 250 copies. Fcap. 8vo.
3s. net. [*Transferred to the
present Publisher.*

Lefroy (Edward Cracroft.)

POEMS. With a Memoir by W. A.
GILL, and a reprint of Mr. J. A.
SYMONDS' Critical Essay on
"Echoes from Theocritus." Cr.
8vo. Photogravure Portrait. 5s.
net.

Le Gallienne (Richard).

PROSE FANCIES. With Portrait of
the Author by WILSON STEER.
Crown 8vo. Purple cloth. 5s.
net. [*Fourth Edition.*
Also a limited large paper edition.
12s. 6d. net.

THE BOOK BILLS OF NARCISSUS.
An Account rendered by RICHARD
LE GALLIENNE. With a Frontispiece. Crown 8vo, purple cloth.
3s. 6d. net. [*Third Edition.*
Also 50 copies on large paper. 8vo.
10s. 6d. net.

ROBERT LOUIS STEVENSON, AN
ELEGY, AND OTHER POEMS,
MAINLY PERSONAL. With Etched
Title-page by D. Y. CAMERON.
Crown 8vo, purple cloth. 4s. 6d.
net.
Also 75 copies on large paper. 8vo.
12s. 6d. net.

ENGLISH POEMS. Crown 8vo, purple cloth. 4s. 6d. net.
[*Fourth Edition, revised.*

GEORGE MEREDITH : Some Char-
acteristics. With a Bibliography
(much enlarged) by JOHN LANE,
portrait, &c. Crown 8vo, purple
cloth. 5s. 6d. net.
[*Fourth Edition.*

Le Gallienne (Richard)—
continued.

THE RELIGION OF A LITERARY
MAN. Crown 8vo, purple cloth.
3s. 6d. net. [*Fifth Thousand.*
Also a special rubricated edition on
hand-made paper. 8vo. 10s. 6d. net.

RETROSPECTIVE REVIEWS, A LITER-
ARY LOG, 1891-1895. 2 vols.
Crown 8vo, purple cloth. 9s.
net.

PROSE FANCIES (Second Series).
Crown 8vo, Purple cloth. 5s. net.

THE QUEST OF THE GOLDEN GIRL.
Crown 8vo. 5s. net.

See also HAZLITT, WALTON and
COTTON.

Lowry (H. D.).

MAKE BELIEVE. Illustrated by
CHARLES ROBINSON. Crown 8vo,
gilt edges or uncut. 5s. net.

WOMEN'S TRAGEDIES. (*See* KEY-
NOTES SERIES).

THE HAPPY EXILE. (*See* ARCADY
LIBRARY).

Lucas (Winifred).

UNITS : Poems. Fcap. 8vo. 3s. 6d.
net.

Lynch (Hannah).

THE GREAT GALEOTO AND FOLLY
OR SAINTLINESS. Two Plays,
from the Spanish of JOSÉ ECHE-
GARAY, with an Introduction.
Small 4to. 5s. 6d. net.

Marzials (Theo.).

THE GALLERY OF PIGEONS AND
OTHER POEMS. Post 8vo. 4s. 6d.
net. [*Transferred to the present
Publisher.*

The Mayfair Set.

Each volume fcap. 8vo. 3s. 6d. net.
I. THE AUTOBIOGRAPHY OF A
BOY. Passages selected by
his friend G. S. STREET.
With a Title-page designed
by C. W. FURSE.
[*Fifth Edition.*
II. THE JONESES AND THE
ASTERISKS. A Story in
Monologue. By GERALD
CAMPBELL. With a Title-
page and 6 Illustrations by
F. H. TOWNSEND.
[*Second Edition.*

The Mayfair Set—*continued.*

III. SELECT CONVERSATIONS WITH AN UNCLE, NOW EXTINCT. By H. G. WELLS. With a Title-page by F. H. TOWNSEND.

IV. FOR PLAIN WOMEN ONLY. By GEORGE FLEMING. With a Title-page by PATTEN WILSON.

V. THE FEASTS OF AUTOLYCUS: THE DIARY OF A GREEDY WOMAN. Edited by ELIZABETH ROBINS PENNELL. With a Title-page by PATTEN WILSON.

VI. MRS. ALBERT GRUNDY: OBSERVATIONS IN PHILISTIA. By HAROLD FREDERIC. With a Title-page by PATTEN WILSON.
[*Second Edition.*

Meredith (George).

THE FIRST PUBLISHED PORTRAIT OF THIS AUTHOR, engraved on the wood by W. BISCOMBE GARDNER, after the painting by G. F. WATTS. Proof copies on Japanese vellum, signed by painter and engraver. £1 1s. net.

Meynell (Mrs.).

POEMS. Fcap. 8vo. 3s. 6d. net.
[*Fifth Edition.*

THE RHYTHM OF LIFE AND OTHER ESSAYS. Fcap. 8vo. 3s. 6d. net.
[*Fifth Edition.*

THE COLOUR OF LIFE AND OTHER ESSAYS. Fcap 8vo. 3s. 6d. net.
[*Fifth Edition.*

THE CHILDREN. Fcap. 8vo. 3s. 6d. net.
[*Second Edition.*

Miller (Joaquin).

THE BUILDING OF THE CITY BEAUTIFUL. Fcap. 8vo. With a Decorated Cover. 5s. net.

Money-Coutts (F. B.).

POEMS. With Title-page designed by PATTEN WILSON. Crown 8vo. 3s. 6d. net.

Monkhouse (Allan).

BOOKS AND PLAYS: A Volume of Essays on Meredith, Borrow, Ibsen, and others. Crown 8vo. 5s. net.

A DELIVERANCE. (*See* KEYNOTES SERIES.)

Nesbit (E.).

A POMANDER OF VERSE. With a Title-page and Cover designed by LAURENCE HOUSMAN. Crown 8vo. 5s. net.

IN HOMESPUN. (*See* KEYNOTES SERIES.)

Nettleship (J. T.).

ROBERT BROWNING: Essays and Thoughts. Crown 8vo. 5s. 6d. net. [*Third Edition.*

Noble (Jas. Ashcroft).

THE SONNET IN ENGLAND AND OTHER ESSAYS. Title-page and Cover Design by AUSTIN YOUNG. Crown 8vo. 5s. net.

Also 50 copies large paper 12s. 6d. net

Oppenheim (Michael).

A HISTORY OF THE ADMINISTRATION OF THE ROYAL NAVY, and of Merchant Shipping in relation to the Navy from MDIX to MDCLX, with an introduction treating of the earlier period. With Illustrations. Demy 8vo. 15s. net.

O'Shaughnessy (Arthur).

HIS LIFE AND HIS WORK. With Selections from his Poems. By LOUISE CHANDLER MOULTON. Portrait and Cover Design. Fcap. 8vo. 5s. net.

Oxford Characters.

A series of lithographed portraits by WILL ROTHENSTEIN, with text by F. YORK POWELL and others. 200 copies only, folio, buckram. £3 3s. net.

25 special large paper copies containing proof impressions of the portraits signed by the artist, £6 6s. net.

Peters (Wm. Theodore).

POSIES OUT OF RINGS. With Title-page by PATTEN WILSON. Sq. 16mo. 2s. 6d. net.

Pierrot's Library.

Each volume with Title-page, Cover and End Papers, designed by AUBREY BEARDSLEY. Sq. 16mo. 2s. net.

I. PIERROT. By H. DE VERE STACPOOLE.
II. MY LITTLE LADY ANNE. By MRS. EGERTON CASTLE.
III. SIMPLICITY. By A. T. G. PRICE.
IV. MY BROTHER. By VINCENT BROWN.

The following are in preparation:

V. DEATH, THE KNIGHT, AND THE LADY. By H. DE VERE STACPOOLE.
VI. MR. PASSINGHAM. By THOMAS COBB.
VII. TWO IN CAPTIVITY. By VINCENT BROWN.

Plarr (Victor).

IN THE DORIAN MOOD: Poems. With Title-page by PATTEN WILSON. Crown 8vo. 5s. net.

Posters in Miniature: over

250 reproductions of French, English and American Posters with Introduction by EDWARD PENFIELD. Large crown 8vo. 5s. net.

Radford (Dollie).

SONGS AND OTHER VERSES. With a Title-page by PATTEN WILSON. Fcap. 8vo. 4s. 6d. net.

Rhys (Ernest).

A LONDON ROSE AND OTHER RHYMES. With Title-page designed by SELWYN IMAGE. Crown 8vo. 5s. net.

Robertson (John M.).

ESSAYS TOWARDS A CRITICAL METHOD. (New Series.) Crown 8vo. 5s. net. [*In preparation.*

St. Cyres (Lord).

THE LITTLE FLOWERS OF ST. FRANCIS: A new rendering into English of the Fioretti di San Francesco. Crown 8vo. 5s. net. [*In preparation.*

Seaman (Owen).

THE BATTLE OF THE BAYS. Fcap. 8vo. 3s. 6d. net.

Sedgwick (Jane Minot).

SONGS FROM THE GREEK. Fcap. 8vo. 3s. 6d. net.

Setoun (Gabriel).

THE CHILD WORLD: Poems. With over 200 Illustrations by CHARLES ROBINSON. Crown 8vo, gilt edges or uncut. 5s. net.

Sharp (Evelyn).

WYMPS: Fairy Tales. With Coloured Illustrations by MABEL DEARMER. Small 4to, decorated cover. 4s. 6d. net.

AT THE RELTON ARMS. (*See* KEYNOTES SERIES.)

THE MAKING OF A PRIG. (*See* FOUR-AND-SIXPENNY NOVELS.)

Shore (Louisa).

POEMS. With an appreciation by FREDERIC HARRISON and a Portrait. Fcap. 8vo. 5s. net.

Short Stories Series.

Each volume Post 8vo. Coloured edges. 2s. 6d. net.

I. SOME WHIMS OF FATE. By MÉNIE MURIEL DOWIE.
II. THE SENTIMENTAL VIKINGS. By R. V. RISLEY.
III. SHADOWS OF LIFE. By Mrs. MURRAY HICKSON.

Stevenson (Robert Louis).

PRINCE OTTO. A Rendering in French by EGERTON CASTLE. With Frontispiece, Title-page, and Cover Design by D. Y. CAMERON. Crown 8vo. 7s. 6d. net.

Also 50 copies on large paper, uniform in size with the Edinburgh Edition of the Works.

A CHILD'S GARDEN OF VERSES. With over 150 Illustrations by CHARLES ROBINSON. Crown 8vo. 5s. net. [*Second Edition.*

Stimson (F. J.)

KING NOANETT. A Romance of Devonshire Settlers in New England. Illustrated. Large crown 8vo. 5s. net.

Stoddart (Thos. Tod).

THE DEATH WAKE. With an Introduction by ANDREW LANG. Fcap. 8vo. 5s. net.

Street (G. S.).

EPISODES. Post 8vo. 3s. net.

MINIATURES AND MOODS. Fcap. 8vo. 3s. net. [*Both transferred to the present Publisher.*

QUALES EGO: A FEW REMARKS, IN PARTICULAR AND AT LARGE. Fcap. 8vo. 3s. 6d. net.

THE AUTOBIOGRAPHY OF A BOY. (*See* MAYFAIR SET.)

THE WISE AND THE WAYWARD. (*See* FOUR - AND - SIXPENNY NOVELS.)

Swettenham (F. A.)

MALAY SKETCHES. With a Title-page and Cover Design by PATTEN WILSON. Crown 8vo. 5s. net.
[*Second Edition.*

Tabb (John B.).

POEMS. Sq. 32mo. 4s. 6d. net.

Tennyson (Frederick).

POEMS OF THE DAY AND YEAR. With a Title-page designed by PATTEN WILSON. Crown 8vo. 5s. net.

Thimm (Carl A.).

A COMPLETE BIBLIOGRAPHY OF FENCING AND DUELLING, AS PRACTISED BY ALL EUROPEAN NATIONS FROM THE MIDDLE AGES TO THE PRESENT DAY. With a Classified Index, arranged Chronologically according to Languages. Illustrated with numerous Portraits of Ancient and Modern Masters of the Art. Title-pages and Frontispieces of some of the earliest works. Portrait of the Author by WILSON STEER, and Title page designed by PATTEN WILSON. 4to. 21s. net.

Thompson (Francis)

POEMS. With Frontispiece, Title-page, and Cover Design by LAURENCE HOUSMAN. Pott 4to. 5s. net. [*Fourth Edition.*

SISTER-SONGS: An Offering to Two Sisters. With Frontispiece, Title-page, and Cover Design by LAURENCE HOUSMAN. Pott 4to. 5s. net.

Thoreau (Henry David).

POEMS OF NATURE. Selected and edited by HENRY S. SALT and FRANK B. SANBORN, with a Title-page designed by PATTEN WILSON. Fcap. 8vo. 4s. 6d. net.

Traill (H. D.).

THE BARBAROUS BRITISHERS: A Tip-top Novel. With Title and Cover Design by AUBREY BEARDSLEY. Crown 8vo, wrapper. 1s. net.

FROM CAIRO TO THE SOUDAN FRONTIER. With Cover Design by PATTEN WILSON. Crown 8vo. 5s. net.

Tynan Hinkson (Katharine)

CUCKOO SONGS. With Title-page and Cover Design by LAURENCE HOUSMAN. Fcap. 8vo. 5s. net.

MIRACLE PLAYS. OUR LORD'S COMING AND CHILDHOOD. With 6 Illustrations, Title-page, and Cover Design by PATTEN WILSON. Fcap. 8vo. 4s. 6d. net.

Walton and Cotton.

THE COMPLEAT ANGLER. Edited by RICHARD LE GALLIENNE. Illustrated by EDMUND H, NEW. Fcap. 4to, decorated cover. 15s. net.

Also to be had in thirteen 1s. parts.

Watson (Rosamund Marriott).

VESPERTILIA AND OTHER POEMS. With a Title-page designed by R. ANNING BELL. Fcap. 8vo. 4s. 6d. net.

A SUMMER NIGHT AND OTHER POEMS. New Edition. With a Decorative Title-page. Fcap. 8vo. 3s. net.

Watson (William).

THE FATHER OF THE FOREST AND OTHER POEMS. With New Photogravure Portrait of the Author Fcap. 8vo, buckram. 3s. 6d. net.
[*Fifth Edition.*

ODES AND OTHER POEMS. Fcap. 8vo, buckram. 4s. 6d. net.
[*Fourth Edition.*

Watson (William)—*continued.*

THE ELOPING ANGELS: A Caprice
Square 16mo, buckram. 3s. 6d.
net.   [*Second Edition.*

EXCURSIONS IN CRITICISM: being
some Prose Recreations of a
Rhymer. Crown 8vo, buckram.
5s. net.   [*Second Edition.*

THE PRINCE'S QUEST AND OTHER
POEMS. With a Bibliographical
Note added. Fcap. 8vo, buckram.
4s. 6d. net.   [*Third Edition.*

THE PURPLE EAST: A Series of
Sonnets on England's Desertion
of Armenia. With a Frontispiece
after G. F. WATTS, R.A. Fcap.
8vo, wrappers. 1s. net.
                [*Third Edition.*

THE YEAR OF SHAME. With an
Introduction by the BISHOP OF
HEREFORD. Fcap. 8vo. 2s. 6d.
net.   [*Second Edition.*

Watt (Francis).

THE LAW'S LUMBER ROOM. Fcap.
8vo. 3s. 6d. net.
                [*Second Edition.*

Watts-Dunton (Theodore).
POEMS. Crown 8vo. 5s. net.
                [*In preparation.*
There will also be an *Edition de Luxe* of
this volume printed at the Kelmscott
Press.

Wenzell (A. B.)
IN VANITY FAIR. 70 Drawings.
Oblong folio. 15s. net.

Wharton (H. T.)
SAPPHO. Memoir, Text, Selected
Renderings, and a Literal Trans-
lation by HENRY THORNTON
WHARTON. With 3 Illustra-
tions in Photogravure, and a
Cover designed by AUBREY
BEARDSLEY. Fcap. 8vo. 7s. 6d.
net.   [*Third Edition.*

THE YELLOW BOOK

An Illustrated Quarterly.

Pott 4to. 5s. net.